THE DEATHDAY
LETTER

THE DEATHDAY
LETTER

Shaun David Hutchinson

Simon Pulse
New York   London   Toronto   Sydney

SIMON PULSE

An imprint of Simon & Schuster Children's Publishing Division
1230 Avenue of the Americas, New York, NY 10020
First Simon Pulse paperback edition June 2010
Copyright © 2010 by Shaun David Hutchinson
All rights reserved, including the right of reproduction
in whole or in part in any form.
SIMON PULSE and colophon are registered trademarks of Simon & Schuster, Inc.
For information about special discounts for bulk purchases, please contact
Simon & Schuster Special Sales at 1-866-506-1949
or business@simonandschuster.com.
The Simon & Schuster Speakers Bureau can bring authors to your live event.
For more information or to book an event contact the Simon & Schuster Speakers
Bureau at 1-866-248-3049 or visit our website at www.simonspeakers.com.
Designed by Mike Rosamilia
The text of this book was set in Berling.
Manufactured in the United States of America
2 4 6 8 10 9 7 5 3 1
Library of Congress Cataloging-in-Publication Data
Hutchinson, Shaun David.
The deathday letter / by Shaun David Hutchinson—1st Simon Pulse
pbk. ed.
p. cm.
Summary: After receiving the letter that says he will be dead within
twenty-four hours, fifteen-year-old Ollie and his two best friends,
Shane and would-be girlfriend Ronnie, set out to fulfill as many
of Ollie's hopes as they can.
ISBN 978-1-4169-9608-8 (pbk.)
ISBN 978-1-4169-9671-2 (eBook)
[1. Death—Fiction. 2. Friendship—Fiction. 3. Dating
(Social customs)—Fiction. 4. Florida—Fiction.] I. Title.
PZ7.H96183De 2010   [Fic]—dc22   2009038697

For Mom, who gave me the tools to succeed,
the stubbornness to never give up,
and for inspiring me every day.

Now where's my lemon meringue pie?

INTRO

The first thing you need to know about Oliver Travers is that at the end of this story he's going to die. There's no twist of fate that saves him, no *deus ex machina*, no deal with the devil that changes what's inevitably going to occur. He's going to croak, and that's just how it is.

But this story isn't about Oliver Travers's death, it's about his life, and the best person to tell that story is Oliver.

23:59 AND COUNTING

Oliver! Oliver, I need you downstairs right now!"

Listen, the last thing I want while I'm doing my part for population control is to hear my mom's voice. It's like a song I can't get out of my head. But here I am, *MMMBop*pin' it under my warm covers before anyone else is supposed to be awake, and she has to go and call my name. I stop and wait, hoping she'll think I'm still asleep. But I may as well put the wookiee down 'cause I know the next time I close my eyes, she'll be there floating around the backs of my eyelids, with her blond hair flyin' and her pink terry cloth bathrobe open just a little more than it should be, telling me to get my lazy butt out of bed or I'll be late for school. And dudes, that just ain't cool.

My mom has a wicked sixth sense for everything except *that*. The woman's a human lie detector and can sense a bad report card from across town, but she still doesn't get what a fifteen-year-old could possibly be doing in the shower for thirty minutes.

Annoyed, I abandon my awesomely warm comforter and shuffle to the bathroom for my morning ritual, which involves taking a leak, brushing my teeth, and attacking my guyfro with a brush. Seriously, I can go from dead asleep to ready in like six point five seconds. I'm sure it's a record.

Once ready, I descend the stairs into the deranged, half-baked circus that is the Travers family.

Mom's the ringleader and lion tamer and even the clown, though I don't think that part's intentional. None of us are really morning people so Mom makes sure we all get where we need to be and that no one dies in the process. She only occasionally has to use the whip.

Dad's like the blind guy who throws the knives at the hot chick on the spinning rack. He wanders around in this funky stupor, running into walls and knocking over chairs, until it's time to throw the knives—then he's a genius. The same goes for his cooking, so long as he has his coffee. God help you if he tries to cook precoffee. Or throw knives.

Obviously, my twin sisters, Edith and Angela, are the freaks.

And Nana? I don't know where she fits in. Do circuses usually have a deceptively sweet puppet master who can wrap you around her pinkie finger with a look and a chocolate chip cookie?

Oh, I forgot about me. Well, when I'm not running crazy late for first period, I'm trying to finish some last-minute project that I've probably had three months to do but have waited until the absolute last possible second to finish. I guess I sort of do my best work under pressure. Like the tightrope walker or that freak that gets shot out of a cannon . . . I wonder if Mom will let me have a cannon.

So you can see it, right? My house is barely controlled chaos in the morning. Okay, it's barely controlled chaos *all* the time, but especially in the morning. Which is why I'm so confused as I walk down the stairs.

I expect to be mowed down by a barrage of motherly advice about staying up too late playing Halo with Shane. Instead, my entire family is gathered around the kitchen table. Mom, Dad, and Nana are standing like curved fishing poles heavy with a catch, while my evil twin sisters are stunned statues on tippy-toes.

And they're all staring at something.

"Oliver Aaron Travers!" yells my mom without turning around.

Mom rarely uses my whole name, mostly 'cause she hates reminding herself that my initials spell "oat." But even if she hadn't yelled my whole name loud enough to make my ears bleed, I can tell by the tone in her voice that something's up.

"Right here, Ma," I say. "You know, yelling in the morning's bad for your blood pressure."

Have you ever had one of those dreams where you're wandering around doing your thing? Maybe you're in the library or school, but you're good, the world's good, everything's good, until you walk into a room and every single person turns to stare at you? And not like one person turns and then the others turn, but every single person turns in unison, like it's some sort of synchronized swimming event? And that's the exact moment you realize you're completely buck-ass naked? Well, I'm not naked, but, you know, I might as well be.

"What?" I say way harsher than I mean to, and immediately feel bad.

There's a millisecond of shocked silence and then, as if on cue, Edith and Angela start bawling. Now I'm certain that something is up. My sisters are the undisputed champions of the universe when it comes to fake crying. It's one of their villainous superpowers because when they turn on their fat, squishy tears and shaky lower lips, there's hardly a person with a soul who can say no to them. But I know them well enough to tell the difference, and these tears are genuine.

I've spent a lot of time asking God how he managed to pack so much pure evil into such adorable little packages. They've got my mom's blond hair and dimples and no one's ever actually caught them doing anything wrong. But it can't be a coincidence that every baby-sitter they've ever had has joined a nunnery or moved to Canada.

"What's wrong? What's going on?" I ask.

Mom's shielding whatever's on the table with her body and I see Dad give her the Look. I get the Look a lot. Usually it's after I've done something stupid like forget to tell Mom that I volunteered her to bake a few dozen cookies for the homecoming bake sale. The Look is Dad's not so subtle way of saying that I better own up to whatever I've done, 'cause it'll hurt worse the longer I put it off. I've never seen the Look directed at Mom though, and she shakes her head in this tense little way that makes her appear as though she's having a seizure.

After an uncomfortable stare-down between Mom and Dad, Mom finally turns to me, and she's crying too. Or she was, anyway. Her nose is clown red and tear tracks run down her face. Mom tries to hide it from me, but she's not nearly as good at hiding her emotions as she thinks she is. Either way, I know it's bad. But it's not until she moves out of the way that I realize there isn't a word for how awful it really is.

It's a Deathday Letter.

Crap.

It's unmistakable. That long white envelope with its goofy rainbow in the corner, as if that can take the sting out of maybe the worst news ever. But come on, if you wrap up a steaming pile of crap in a pink bow, it's still a steaming pile of crap.

I'm shocked, and everyone seems to be waiting to move until they see how I'm going to react. I don't know what makes me do it, but I run to Nana and throw my arms around her.

"I'm so sorry, Nana," I say as I try to bury my head in her shoulder like I did when I was a kid. Only it doesn't work so well, 'cause I've grown and she's shrunk. "I don't want you to die."

Nana's my favorite person in the whole world. Honestly. She's seventy-eight years of awesome in this tiny, wrinkly body. You'd never know she's as old as Methuselah by the way she runs around. Not only does she still teach tennis to all the neighborhood kids, she's the only person in my family I can talk to about girls without wanting to gnaw my arm off in abject embarrassment. Dad got her to move in after my Grandpa Lou died by telling her he needed help with the twins (which wasn't far from the truth). I don't know how I'll make it without her. All I know, as I hug her tighter than I've hugged her in ages, is that I don't want her to die.

Nana grabs me by my shoulders and pushes me out to arm's length. "What makes you think the letter belongs to me?"

I stop myself from saying, "Because you're older than paper," and look at my parents. "Mom? Dad? Which one of you is it? I can't lose either of you." My whole world is slowly crumbling around me. If it's not Nana, then it's got to be one of them. It can't be one of the twins, 'cause my family wouldn't have waited for me to come downstairs to have their freak-out. But it can't be Mom or Dad either. Without Mom I'd never get to school on time or know if my underwear is clean. Without Dad I'd never know . . . well I'd probably never have anyone to watch crappy movies with again. Losing either of them is too much to handle.

Nana sobs and snorts behind me and isn't holding it together any better than the twins, who are still bawling—they're a testament to the superior lung capacity of nine-year-old girls. Nana's crying so hard I assume the Deathday Letter has got to be Dad's. Don't get me wrong, Nana loves Mom, but she told me once that she sometimes wishes Dad had married his high school sweetheart, Lily Purdy. Lily was a redhead and Nana always wanted redheaded grandkids.

"Ollie," says Dad. "I think you should look at it." It's kind of unsettling for my dad to be the one who's calm and in control. Plus, he only ever calls me Ollie when we're having one of our man-to-man talks, like the time he tried to talk to me about girls. He said, "Ollie, girls are like trees you have to climb. No. Wait. Girls are like vending machines that you have to keep stocked. And when you want something, you have to give them money. Wait, that's not right. Ollie, forget what I just said. Girls are like Tetris. You have to line everything up just right to get them to go down—" It got even worse after that. He used the word "plumbing." Twice. So Dad's steady, even tone is scarier than what's on the table, and I'm at a total loss.

People get Deathday Letters all the time. Your mom, your dad, teachers, that guy you saw on the interstate with his finger buried in his nose to the second knuckle. Everyone gets one. And once it shows up—*bam*—the twenty-four-hour countdown to death begins. It's not exactly twenty-four hours but it's close enough. It's the worst kind of letter you can possibly get, but I can't imagine what the world would be like if people *didn't* get them. Scary.

The letter on the table isn't even the first one I've ever seen. My grandpa and I had been really close. He'd gotten me into building model rockets and we'd sit for hours putting them together. Grandpa Lou loved everyone, but I was his favorite. After he died, I sneaked into his room and stole his letter. I know it's selfish to steal something that Dad probably wanted to keep but I'm pretty sure Grandpa Lou would have wanted me to have it.

But the letter on the table doesn't have Grandpa Lou's name on it or Nana's or even Mom's or Dad's. Written neatly on the front of the envelope in a slanted, loopy script is:

Oliver Aaron Travers

I don't really believe it because I immediately snatch it up and dig my finger under the sealed flap, wondering as I do whose crappy job it is to lick these things. It reads:

October 16

Mr. Oliver Aaron Travers,

It is our duty to inform you that your death is scheduled to occur tomorrow in the early morning hours of October 17th.

Your cooperation in this matter is greatly appreciated. Have a pleasant Deathday!

"Umm, okay." Yes. That *is* my response to finding out I'm living-challenged. My parents obviously expect me to be a lot more broken up than I am, 'cause they rush me and start hugging me and messing my hair, which is already a natural disaster and doesn't need their help.

"Ollie, I love you so much," says Mom. "Girls, tell your brother you love him."

"We love you, Ollie," say my sisters. They've mostly stopped crying and are moving on. Trust me, the fact that I got tears out of them at all is kind of a minor miracle. Dude, seriously, one day my sisters are gonna grow up to be crazy successful lawyers or hit women. I'm keeping my fingers crossed for assassins, 'cause how cool would *that* be?

Nana pushes Mom and my sisters out of the way, which is the sort of thing only she can get away with. "I'm sorry, Oliver, I wish it *had* been my letter."

"No you don't, Nana," I tell her, and flash her one of my crooked, toothy smiles she claims she loves so much. When people talk about a smile only a (grand)mother could love, they're absolutely talking about mine.

"Honesty isn't always a pretty quality, Oliver." Nana smiles back at me. Her face is kind of puffy, and her wrinkly skin hangs like limp turkey flesh. But when she smiles, it's like a thousand years evaporate right off her face. "You're right though," she whispers in my ear. "I still have a few good years of annoying your mother left in these old bones."

How could anyone not love someone like her?

"Well, I'm hungry," I say as I disentangle myself from Nana. In the kerfuffle, Mom's forgotten to do anything about breakfast, and I'm starving. I'm always starving, actually.

Listen, there are four things in life you can always count on. One and two you already know: taxes and Deathday Letters. But the others you might not know.

The third immutable law of life is that guys really do spend 99.999 percent of their (waking and sleeping) lives thinking about sex. Sitting in a church? Thinking about sex. Being forced to sit through a World War II documentary? Thinking about sex. Mowing the lawn? Thinking about sex.

The last fact of life is that guys are always hungry. Even when we say we're not, we can totally eat. I think it's like a hunting instinct left over from a billion years ago when dudes wore bearskins and drew on cave walls. See, a guy who isn't hungry has no real incentive to go out and hunt food for the clan, 'cause we're lazy, too. Add that to the list: taxes, Deathday Letters, guys have sex on the brain, are always hungry, and are lazy. I mean, imagine a Neanderthal dude in the dinosaur times, not hungry, sitting around the cave, watching the wall, saying, "I'm not really hungry. I'll go hunting tomorrow." Especially if there's a football game on the wall.

So I'm definitely hungry and there's nothing to eat.

"What do you want?" asks Dad. "I'll make anything." Then he starts running around the kitchen throwing pots and pans everywhere, which really pisses Mom off. And, since he hasn't had his coffee, he's a one-man wrecking machine wrecking all Mom's stuff.

"Whatever it is, you gotta make it fast," I say. "I have to get to school."

"Don't be silly," says Mom. "You're not going to school."

"Not fair!" cries Edith.

"If he doesn't have to go, then neither do we," finishes Angela.

Nana strokes their heads and says, "If anyone's going to school, it's you two."

"I'm going to school," I tell them. "I mean, I'm not gonna sit around here all day. Nana's got lessons, Dad's got the restaurant, and you have mom stuff to do."

Dad looks up from the bottom cabinets. "But aren't there things you want to do? The whole day is yours."

The naked feeling creeps over me again. It's like they're waiting for me to spill all my deep dark dreams out onto the floor for them to rifle through.

Dear Diary,

When I grow up, I want to be a ballerina.

"Seriously, guys, you're creeping me out. My life's been good. Really. I think I've pretty much done all the stuff I wanted. I mean, I'm never gonna pitch for the Yankees but even in my dreams that was never gonna happen. I think I just want to go to school and do normal stuff." They're all still staring at me so I say, "This isn't a big deal, you know."

Of course it's a big deal! Just not the kind I want to go through under the glassy, teary, snotty stares of my family.

"If he's going to school," begins Angela.

"Can we stay home in his place?" Edith finishes. Then they both smile. You'd think the first skill they'd teach minions of evil at the Evil Academy for Evil Girls would be how to smile without looking like the demon-possessed girl from *The Exorcist* (watched it, thought about sex).

"No," say Mom, Dad, and Nana at the exact same moment. It's funny because I know my mom and Nana are both immune to their powers, but I've seen my dad melt way too many times under the fiery heat of their pouty lips and droopy eyes.

Edgy silence follows while Dad makes scrambled eggs. The problem with that sentence is that my dad is utterly incapable of making plain old scrambled eggs, so he carpet bombs them with every vegetable in the fridge and every spice in the cabinet. I know that in some dark corner of his noncaffeinated brain, celery seems like a fantastic idea, but the execution makes me wanna be executed. Or, you know, not.

On top of having to eat the universe's most disgusting scrambled eggs, I can sense my family having this silent dialogue that goes a little something like this:

That's the last bite of egg Ollie's ever going to eat.

That's the last time Ollie's ever going to slurp his orange juice.

That's the last time he's ever going to get yelled at for belching at the table.

That's the last time Ollie's not going to use his napkin.

Except for my sisters, who are still plotting how to use my Deathday Letter to either get themselves out of school or get ponies. I put my odds on the ponies. Plus they'll make the coolest pony-mounted assassins in the fourth grade, taking out math teachers for Pez.

Finally, I've had enough. "Guys!" I yell. "Stop acting like I'm gonna die."

Mom stops dancing nervously around the kitchen, making lists of things she wants to buy for dinner. Nana stops flipping through her photo albums, looking at pictures of me like I'm already gone. And Dad stops stirring the toxic sludge formerly known as hash browns.

"Ollie," says Nana. "You *are* going to die."

I know that everyone's thinking it, and I love Nana for having the balls to say it. Of course, that doesn't mean I'm ready to go coffin shopping.

"Maybe, but you don't have to act like it." I push away the plate and hunt for my backpack. The twins love hiding it, but there are only so many places they can hide a backpack heavy enough to give me scoliosis.

"Oliver—," begins Dad.

"Everyone gets a Deathday Letter!" I yell again. I don't mean to yell, but sometimes yelling just happens. I count to ten and try again . . . without the yelling. "At some point, everyone gets a letter. My life's been pretty solid and I don't want to spend my last day locked in this house while you all stare at me, waiting for me to drop dead. I want to go to school, hang with my friends, come home, and try to ignore you all until I go to bed. The only difference between this day and any other day is that I won't have to worry about making up an excuse for why I didn't do my homework. Okay?"

Wow. That sucked, but it had to be said. And I know they get the point because Mom starts yelling at the twins, who haven't brushed their hair yet—likely hoping that she'll cave and let them stay home. Nana's already reading the paper like normal, which means she's brutalizing it. It's a crinkly black and white bloodbath. Oh, and Dad goes back to terrorizing more eggs. I don't know whether to feel worse for the newspaper or the eggs.

"You're going to be late," says Mom. She looks at me out of the corner of her eye and I know it's eating her up not being able to cry and hover and mother the crap out of me, but I'm not about to stay home and watch *Oprah* all day.

I get ready to leave, and maybe my sisters have just a sliver of humanity between them, because I find my backpack sitting in front of the door.

I know everyone's pretending and it makes me feel like a real dick. I also know that the second I leave, the crying and moping will resume. And since I'm not a total douche, I give each of them a hug before I leave. Even my sisters.

"Here," says Dad, and he hands me a wad of cash. "For lunch."

I look down at the money. School lunch, which Dad abhors, is only about five bucks, but he's given me enough for, like, sixty lunches. "What's this for?"

Dad shrugs and winks at me. "You never know where the day might take you."

"Actually, I do," I say. "First period is History, then Alge—"

"I swear, if you didn't have my good looks, I'd think you were the garbageman's son." Dad chuckles and closes my hand around the money. "You'll figure it out. Now go or you'll be late."

The whole thing is kind of surreal, but Dad's right about being late. And you know, there *is* a giant neon sign above my head flashing, FOR A LIMITED TIME ONLY.

Getting out of my house is probably for the best, even if the only alternative is school. I hate Moriville High but it's where the girls are. And girls equal sex, which, even though I've never technically done it, is sort of my whole reason for being. I can pass an entire period of Mr. Barnes's history class just staring at Miranda Hilley's rack. It makes me want to plant a flag in it and claim it in the name of Ollie. Of course, when I say "flag," I mean "my face."

Girls are lucky 'cause they get points for showing off their assets. I, on the other hand, have to wear the baggiest jeans I own in case my bald avenger decides to turn into a rock python at the exact moment Mrs. Keane decides I need to solve for x in front of the whole class. It's a lot of pressure for a guy. All I have to do is rub a wall the wrong way and I'm perpendicular. Ever wonder why so many dudes sit in the back of class and act like they don't know what's going on? Because a teenage guy with a penis is like a twitchy marine with a live grenade. Got it?

If you're keeping score: I like girls. School is a giant place filled with girls. It's horny math even I can do.

As I walk to my best friend Shane's house, I realize that bringing my backpack was just plain stupid. I don't crack open my books on the days I *am* gonna be alive to take the test. But I don't want to deal with my parents again so I'm stuck with it.

It's cool, I guess, that Shane's a couple months older than me and gets to drive. One awesome perk is that I don't have to ride the bus to school. The bus driver, Dozie, is insane. And I can't prove it, but I'm pretty sure he's legally blind. It'd be nice if Shane would get off his butt and pick me up, but he claims that the extra block is too far out of his way. Which is crap, but he who has the car has the power.

Another perk should be that it helps us out with the girls. It's a simple fact: Girls like boys with cars. Except when the car in question is a rust red '85 Honda Accord named Miss Piggy. Let's just say that the girls aren't exactly shoving one another out of the way for rides. In fact, Marissa Sheldon once told me she'd rather ride home on her ten-year-old brother's handlebars than be seen in Miss Piggy. It puts our cool quotient slightly below the school janitor, Lewis, who buys beer for some of the jocks, and slightly above the girl in the library who eats her own fingernails.

"Are you ever on time?"

I look up and see Shane Grimsley leaning against his car. Waiting.

Shane and I have been best friends since before birth. Literally. My mom and Shane's mom met at their lady doctor. By lady doctor, I don't mean a doctor who's a lady, though she was. I mean a doctor who says things like, "Put your feet in the stirrups," and boldly goes where no dude should ever go on his own mom. Anyway, we were born just a couple months apart.

"So I think I've figured something out, Shane. I think we were switched when we were babies." I stop in front of him and drop my backpack on the sidewalk. It clunks.

"It hurts me when you think, Ollie."

"Just hear me out. I think that one day we were playing together, our moms were having some tasty cocktails, talking about laundry detergent and particle physics, and someone took the wrong baby home. I'm really Shane Grimsley and you're really Oliver Travers."

Shane looks at me like I've shoved a handful of poo in his face and he's taken a huge whiff. And seen some corn. There's always corn.

"Sure," Shane says after a second. "Except, you do remember I'm black, right? My mom's black, my dad's black, my granny and gramps are black." Shane points at himself and his invisible family. "We're *all* black."

I shrug. "So what?"

"You're *not* black. You're the polar opposite of black. You're so white I should probably wear shades."

"Minor details."

I wait for Shane to ask me where I was going with the switched-at-birth thing but instead he pulls his cell phone out of his pocket and flips it open. "So, we're going to be late."

I look at my own phone. "We have time." Yeah, time for me to get all blubbery and tell you about my letter. Except I don't do it. Because I'm chicken. Extra-crispy.

"I'm hungry and in need of unhealthy breakfast sandwiches." Shane walks around to his side of the car. The door *screeee*s as it opens and I feel it in my teeth. "You haven't eaten, have you?"

I give him my crazy look. It's more scary than crazy, with a healthy dose of squinty. "Um, I have, but what's that got to do with the price of sloppy joes on Wednesdays?"

Shane slides into his seat. The upholstery is the color of wet cardboard. "Then what're you waiting on, Travers?" calls Shane. "You know the Grimsleys don't know how to cook anything they don't know the chemical composition of. This belly needs food."

I get in the car and decide to wait to tell Shane. I'm afraid that once I tell him, this will all end and he'll start acting like my parents. Is it so wrong to not want to spend my last day under a microscope?

I put on my seat belt because Shane's car is pretty much held together with happy thoughts and centrifugal force. He figures the faster he goes, the better chance Miss Piggy has of not flying apart. And while I know I'm going to die, I certainly don't want it to be this morning in Shane's crappy car.

I barely hear Shane babbling about Tim Palachik's latest escapade because I'm leaning out the window staring at stuff

I've seen like a million times before. But as we pass each gas station and every crossing guard, I know that it's probably going to be the last time I see them. I'm gonna miss the Country Corner Store's sign advertising FOOT-LONG SPICY WIENERS. Cracks me up every time.

"Did you hear what I said?" asks Shane as we pull into the drive-thru.

"No?"

"I said that Tim said that he made out with Kaylee Sanders. It's all over his CrowFlow page."

Moriville High's mascot is the Great and Mighty Crow. Pretty lame. Even lamer is that we have our own social networking site called CrowFlow. It's like Facebook but without peedos.

While Shane is ordering my bacon, egg, and cheese biscuit, I pull out my phone and check for myself. "Dude," I say as we pull away in a haze of exhaust and painful squeals, "this says Tim *screwed* Kaylee." I make a vulgar hand gesture involving the okay sign and my index finger poking through it to emphasize my point, which probably doesn't need any emphasis.

"Right. Made out." Shane tosses me my sandwich while simultaneously stuffing half of his in his mouth.

"No." I put my phone away. "That's not what 'screwing' implies. Did you not see my visual aid?" I unwrap my steamy breakfast sandwich and hold it on my lap while it cools. "'Screwing' implies panty spelunking. It implies power ballads in the background and grunting in the foreground. It implies playing the front nine. Or the back nine, if you're lucky."

Shane rolls his eyes at me. It's kind of funny because he

wears these thick glasses that make him look all bug-eyed. And when he rolls his eyes, I always expect them to keep rolling and fall right out of his head.

"Remember the time Tim said he made out with Jen Green and it turned out all he'd really done was accidentally brush up against her boob in the hall?"

"Right," I say with a little relief. "The Rule." No matter what you actually do or don't do with a girl, when you tell the story, you have to embellish some, er, a lot. If you kiss a girl, you say you felt her up. If you make out with a girl, you say you did her. And if you ever actually manage to go all the way, well you just have to tell the boys that you ruined her for all mankind. What can I say? Half a dude's brain is in his shorts.

I gulp down my second breakfast and hold on for dear life. Shane doesn't have a stereo in his car. His parents believe that if he's busy listening to the radio, he won't be paying attention to the actual driving. Unfortunately it just forces him to entertain himself in other, more distracting ways.

"So where'd Tim hook up with Kaylee, anyway?" I ask once I'm done chewing. "It's not like they hang out with the same group."

"Party," says Shane.

"How come we never get invited to parties? Just once before I die I'd like to be invited to a party."

Shane snorts. "Not much chance of that."

"You have no idea," I mumble.

"What?"

"Nothing. Just concentrate on the road."

While Shane drives badly and babbles about all the parties we're likely to never be invited to, I stick my head back out the window and breathe in the air. It's a little nipply, but it's not like I'm worried about catching pneumonia. Fall's my favorite part of the year, and not 'cause it's close to my birthday. We don't get much in the way of fall down in Florida. Still, it's the one time of year when people actually celebrate stuff getting old instead of trying to cut it out, cover it up, or stretch it tighter than a snare drum. Age is yellow and red and orange and brown, and I think that makes it kind of awesome.

Before I know it, we're pulling into the underclassmen parking lot and Shane is swearing because we have to park so far in the back.

"Get your bag, Travers," says Shane as I slam the door.

I turn around to get my books but hesitate. "Yeah, I don't think so."

"Completely giving up the pretense of being awake?"

"Something like that." I shrug and start walking. Shane follows.

So school sucks hard, but Mom always made me go so I could get into a "decent college." I guess that doesn't matter anymore. Still, I want to know whose awesomely idiotic idea it was to cram a whole bunch of teenagers into one giant, hermetically sealed bubble and expect us not to kill and devour each other. There's a reason caterpillars go into cocoons to turn into butterflies. Because teenagers are monsters.

My letter is still tucked safely in my front pocket as I walk the halls. Every time Shane looks in my direction I grin and hope that this is all a big mistake. Like maybe I'll find out the letter is meant for another Oliver Aaron Travers.

I wait while Shane gets some stuff out of his locker. He needs his books even less than I do. I don't need mine on account of I'm getting ready to curdle, but Shane can go sans books on account of the kid's a freaking genius. The worst part is that our teachers know it. It's gotta be tough knowing one of your students can teach your class better than you.

Shane's still babbling about some commercial he saw on TV that made him blow soda out of his nose when I see Veronica Dittrich. Ronnie. It's like Hiroshima all over again. In my pants. But she's not just any girl. She's *the* girl.

I should go to first period. I should turn around and run to Mr. Barnes's boring history class. But I don't. Because my eyes are stuck on Ronnie. She walks through the halls like she's the only person in the entire school. At least, that's how I see her. There's music playing—the kind they play in saptastic romcoms—and it's like she's got her own personal wind machine and lighting crew following her around, making her look perfect all the time.

Ronnie looks my way and tries to smile and wave. One of those little down-low things. Real casual. I want to smile back. I want to run across the hall and unbreak up so I can toss her over my shoulder and spend the whole day doing R-rated stuff. Instead, I look like I'm gonna puke. Every girl's dream, right? But I can't help it. I'm frozen and freaked and probably a little green.

Shane grabs my arm and drags me out of the line of fire. I look over my shoulder and watch her stomp away.

Ronnie, Shane, and I had been friends growing up. Best friends. Ronnie had always been one of the guys until one day she turned into a girl. She left eighth grade with microdots and a wicked curveball and came back freshman year with C-cups and a purse.

Don't get me wrong, Ronnie was pretty before. She's got longish brown hair and a pointy nose and eyes and stuff, but it's her girl attributes that turn my brain to oatmeal. Raisin oatmeal.

We dated briefly and then she broke up with me. On our one-week anniversary. I'd made her an iTunes mix and everything. We stopped talking after that. I got possession of Shane and our lunch table, and Ronnie got my balls. Well, that's what Shane says anyway. Most of the time I wish we could all just go back to being friends.

And then I realize Shane's snapping his fingers in front of my face. "Dude," he says. "It's been six weeks. Six weeks since Ronnie dumped you. Six weeks of pathetic, vomit-worthy moping."

"What's your point?"

"You only dated for a week. That's like one week of moping for every day you dated."

"No math before lunch, Shane."

Shane growls. "There are other girls, man. Colleen Wright's totally got it for you."

I stop in the middle of the hall and shove a freshman out of the way. "She's also got a stutter."

Shane wriggles his eyebrows. "She's not the kind of girl you take out for conversation."

"Shane."

"Ollie. I'm your best friend. Trust me, Ronnie is not the girl for you. She dumped you. You need to move on."

"Yeah," I say, knowing he won't leave me alone until he gets his way. "Screw Ronnie." I almost sound like I mean it. There are days I wake up and draw devil horns on Ronnie's picture, and days I look at Ronnie's picture and get a devil horn of my own. It was complicated enough before I found out I'm dying.

The warning bell rings and we file into class. Mr. Barnes's room is like a *Schoolhouse Rock!* parody. There are cartoon animals and giant talking president's heads spouting facts about everything from how many men died in World War I to where Lincoln was when he got his Deathday Letter.

Mr. Barnes is kind of a cartoon too. He's busy chalking it up at the front of the class as Shane and I slide into our seats. He's got this thumb-length ponytail that quivers and bobs as he writes his notes. I feel bad for the guy. His ponytail is about the only hair he has on his head that's not coming out of his nose. Every year at least one student leaves him a nose hair trimmer for Christmas. Funny? Cruel? I guess it depends on which side of the desk you sit.

The bacon, egg, and cheese biscuit swirls around in my stomach, trying to make me fall asleep. Mr. Barnes's voice doesn't help. Being that it's my last day, I try to fight it, but the more Mr. Barnes drones, the more I just want to close my eyes.

Maybe the letter got it wrong. Maybe it's come a day late. Maybe I'm going to die of utter and complete boredom right here in Mr. Barnes's class.

Shane is busy taking notes. I swear it looks like the kid's writing down what Mr. Barnes is saying before Mr. Barnes knows he's gonna say it.

Miranda Hilley's wearing this lime green V-neck thing with a gold cross hanging in the sweaty crease of her boobs. Resurrection indeed.

The seconds move backward. Not even Miranda Hilley's fog lights can make class go by any faster. And yet, as slow as the class is passing, I can feel my last day rushing past me like I'm in a wind tunnel. I can see my parents standing over my grave sobbing, "He went to school!" I can read my own epitaph. It says, OLIVER TRAVERS. HE DIED.

I don't want to die. I want to live.

"*Shane!*" I whisper. Shane stops writing and looks at me over his thick black glasses. Then he steals a glance over at Miranda. He knows there's usually only one reason I'd distract him during class.

"*Nice.*" He starts writing again.

"Shane!"

Shane glares at me and Mr. Barnes looks up, stumbling over the words, "French Indochina." Shane keeps glaring. I've had my hand in my pocket, holding the letter all class. It's damp from my sweat but I clench my fist and toss it onto his desk.

Shane knows what the letter is without having to unfold it. There are people who spend their whole lives searching for the 120-watt incandescent white paper that Deathday Letters are written on. It's unmistakable. Loads of people think it's sick that a letter announcing final boarding on the plane to Deadville comes in a jolly rainbow-printed envelope. They're the same people who think it should be written in blood and come on froufrou, lacy black paper or something. Aside from having my name on it, I think it's perfect.

Shane stares at the letter. Having known the kid as long as I have, I like to think that I know every expression his face can possibly make, but it's making one I've never seen before. It's somewhere between the time he accidentally watched an entire program about tiny flies that burrow into people's scalps and lay eggs, and the time we were playing T-ball and I whacked him in the Wiffle balls with my plastic bat.

I whisper his name again but he ignores me. Minutes pass. I've never seen him this upset. I think maybe I've done it. I've broken Shane Grimsley. And just when I'm about to give up, Shane groans and falls out of his seat.

"My stomach!" Shane cries out. "Mr. Barnes, my stomach!"

I snatch the letter off of his desk and stand up. "Mr. Barnes, I think Shane needs to go to the clinic."

Mr. Barnes is the exact opposite of the kind of person you want around in an emergency. He doesn't move or speak. He just watches Shane squirm around on the ground. I think guys like him spend so much time in the past that they don't know how to act in the present.

Finally, he scribbles a pass and gives it to me. "Go. Go ahead."

I grab Shane's bag, help him up, and rush him out of class. The second the door clicks shut behind us, Shane shoves me away and takes off down the hall.

"Wait up," I call after him. He walks all the way down to the water fountain before stopping. "What the hell's your problem, Shane?"

Let me just say that of all the things I'm expecting my best friend to do at this moment, punching me in the eye isn't one of them. It's so low on the list that it's between writing me a love sonnet and telling me he's a glittery vampire. But that's exactly what he does. Shane Grimsley turns around, pulls back his fist, and coldcocks me right in the eye. Hard. So hard, I fall back a couple of steps. I don't even have time to be in pain before he starts yelling at me.

"Are you kidding me with this? We do everything together! We got the chicken pox together, we downloaded our first porn together—"

"Which was a little weird, by the way." I resist the urge to touch my eye; I don't want to look like a wuss.

Shane's eyes are all whites and I know that talking now is bad. "And we were supposed to go to prom together. Well, not *together* together."

"Yeah, and to Europe together, and college together. Shane, I get it." My eye hurts like Shane's taken a lemon, squeezed out all the pulp, mixed it with some salt, and then used it to punch me in the eye. "But it's a Deathday Letter. It's not like I sent in cereal box tops for it."

"I don't care." Shane paces back and forth across the hall. "You're breaking a blood oath, man. Our oath."

"Shane, that was back in third grade. And it wasn't blood, it was Tabasco."

"Still, you don't break that kind of oath."

I pull the letter out of my pocket. "You think I want to die? If I could, I'd just send this back to wherever it came from and tell them I'm not allowed to die yet, 'cause I swore a Tabasco oath with my best friend."

"Fine!"

"Fine."

Shane squints at me and I brace myself in case he decides to deck me again.

"We cool?" I ask.

Shane picks up his backpack and shoulders it. "I guess staying pissed at you your whole last day would be kind of lame."

"Be pissed at me tomorrow."

"It won't be fun tomorrow." Shane looks up at me and puckers his lips like he's eating something that he can't decide whether to swallow or spit out. He says, "I got you good."

"You punch like a pansy."

"It's going to bruise."

I touch my eye and wince. It already feels like it's five times the normal size. I hope it doesn't bruise too badly, 'cause the last thing I need is to look like I'm playing an extra in a zombie flick *and* like I just got sucker punched by a nerdy black kid with girl hands.

"Can I tell people I was robbed?"

"Why?" Shane raises his eyebrow like it's totally possible he'll punch me out again if I give him the wrong answer.

"Because tomorrow I'll be dead, right? I don't want the last thing people remember about me to be that you kicked my ass."

Shane thinks about it. His thinking face makes him look

gassy. "I guess that's all right. But why tell them you were robbed? Why not tell people that you were in the mall and you saw this totally hot mom getting her purse snatched in the parking lot? You tried to save her, and the guy punched you. You went down like a you-know-what in a you-know-where, and even though the thief got the purse, the mom was *really* grateful."

"Wait. Why do I get my ass kicked and still not manage to keep the hot mom from getting jacked?"

"Not believable." Shane nods like he's imagining the whole thing, which is creepy. "Tell people you got your butt kicked *trying* to save the hot mom, and that she took a little trip south of the border to thank you for the effort. That sounds like something that could actually happen."

"Yeah, on Cinemax After Dark."

Shane claps me on the back. "Listen, I've known you since you were a baby, man. You're like a brother. I know everything there is to know about you, and lots of stuff I wish I didn't. It's not just my job to tell you the truth, it's my obligation."

We stand in silence until finally I say, "What do we do about my letter?" because standing around not talking about our feelings feels way gayer than actually talking about our feelings.

"What do you mean?"

"I'm not going back to class. I already know how the war ends. We won. And I don't want to sit around and cry about my letter."

One of Shane's infamous grins begins to spread over his face like pancake syrup. His grin is usually the cornerstone of a crooked path to trouble. "I'm game for anything, Travers. You tell me how you want to spend your last day, and I'll make it happen. I'm the wizard and you're—"

"I'm not Dorothy."

"You know what I mean. It's your last day, dude."

I shake my head and lean against the wall. "That's just it. I don't want to have a last day. I don't want to die at all."

Shane pats me on the shoulder. "I can't keep you from going out, but I can make sure you go out with a little dignity."

"I can't die, Shane. I thought maybe if I came here, if I did normal shit, that I'd realize it was all some stupid mistake."

"So what?" asks Shane. "You want to go back to class?"

I start to tell Shane that class is the last place I want to be, but once Shane gets going, there's no stopping him.

"No, let's do that. Let's go to class. It'll be sob city. If you live until third period, Señora Schwartz can throw you one of her Deathday fiestas."

"Shane—"

"Oliver," says Shane, mocking me. "Weigh it out, man. On the one hand, you have Señora Schwartz and her stupid Deathday flan and streamers and hats and lots of people who wouldn't spit on you under normal circumstances weeping and telling you how much they'll miss you—"

I have no idea where Shane' s going with this but he's like the Mississippi and I'm just a bit of flotsam. I don't stand a chance. "What's on the other hand, Shane?"

Shane's grin widens. I'm increasingly convinced that he's definitely going to get us into trouble. People don't understand why I hang out with Shane. But it's this—the grin and the big piles of crap we jump into and then always somehow dig our way out of. And I have a feeling that he's handing me a shovel.

"If you trust me," says Shane, "I promise not to get you arrested."

"I guess," I say.

"Let Moriville High be a fondish memory."

Somewhere in the back of my mind, I know Shane's right. I hate school. I'm not ready to die, and Shane's not ready to let me die a boring loser. School has nothing left to offer me.

"Okay, let's go. Maybe we can stop at the store and grab some snacks. We'll eat and play Halo till we yak."

Shane claps me on the back. "Yeah. Um. I don't really have a plan yet, but that lame-ass suggestion isn't going to be anywhere near it."

I start leading the charge out of school when I notice Shane's not behind me. "What?"

"There's one more thing."

"What?"

"I need your letter."

"Shane?"

"Trust me."

I nod and hand Shane my moist letter.

Shane barrels down the hall and it's only when he's standing at the door that I realize where we are. Algebra. Mrs. Alley's class. Ronnie's class.

"Shane, what're you doing?"

Shane's the kind of guy who either does something without thinking at all or spends hours making a pro/con list about whether he'd rather download slutty cheerleaders or slutty ninja girls. Today I think he's thrown all rational thought completely out the window.

He steps up to the window and stares inside. I'm not exactly sure what he's trying to do but he shoos me away when I try to tell him that the fastest way to ruin my Deathday is to bring along Ronnie. I mean, unless the good ship Ronniepop's suddenly started taking passengers, I'm just not in the mood for any of her girly BS.

Finally, as I'm about to give up on Shane and take off on my own, he knocks on the window. *Rap, rap, rap.* Around his ears I see the entire class turn to stare. A second later he takes my Deathday Letter and slams it against the tiny window, holding it there for a count of five before folding it back and handing it to me.

It takes less than thirty seconds for the door to open. Mrs. Alley is shouting something I can't understand but Ronnie ignores her and slams the door shut behind her.

"Where are we going, how long do you have, and more importantly, did you give Ollie that shiner?" she asks without taking a breath.

Shane shakes his head and says, "It's not mine."

Ronnie points at me and, I admit it, I did a little pointing of my own. "Ollie?" she says without looking at me.

"Yeah," I say as noncreepy as I can. "But, you know, you don't have to come along. It was Shane's—"

"So you don't want me here?" Ronnie turns back to Shane. "He doesn't want me—"

"I mean, you can come if you want. I don't care."

Shane rolls his crazy, marble eyes and growls. "Ronnie, you're coming. Ollie, you'll thank me for this tomorrow. Or later today. Whatever. Can we just go before we get busted?"

Ronnie smiles at me. It's the first time all day that I'm not wishing I wasn't on death's most wanted list. If dying's what it takes to get Ronnie back, then I'll be a stiff. You know what I mean.

"Let's do this thing, Grimsley."

Shane isn't just handing me a shovel, he's handing me the keys to a bulldozer.

22:02

"Thbbt pidda ith so goot," says Shane.

"Yeah, awesome." I weave to the side to avoid the spray of marinara. Ronnie does the same thing and gives me a little grin, which, in spite of myself, I almost return. Broken up or not, Ronnie's just about the raddest girl in the universe. Definitely the raddest girl in the kitchen.

"Are you going to eat, Ollie?" asks Ronnie.

The pizza box is spread open on Shane's kitchen island and we hover around it, not unlike vultures.

I love Shane's house. It's a crazy collection of science articles and sticky notes. But since Mr. Grimsley's an honest-to-God rocket scientist and Mrs. Grimsley does something with computers I'm not even sure there's a proper word for, the sticky notes aren't just sticky notes. They're part of a game. One Grimsley starts by putting up a note that has a random piece of information on it. Like 3,134 kelvins. Then the others put up notes guessing what it is. It's the boiling point of iron, by the way.

"I don't really feel like eating right now," I say. I don't really feel like talking either, but since they're both here and tomorrow I won't be, I'm trying to make the best of it.

Shane dribbles mushy bits of mostly chewed pizza as he tries to speak before swallowing. "Since when do *you* not feel like eating?"

"Leave it, Shane," says Ronnie. "It's not even nine in the morning and he's already had two breakfasts."

"That does—," Shane and I say at the same time before we both stop and laugh.

"Go ahead," I say.

Shane shakes his head. "No way, man, it's all you."

"Really, Shane," I say slowly, looking through my eyelashes at Ronnie.

The kid's pretty dense for being a genius, but he finally gets that I'm not ready for a lot of talky time with Ronnie. "You should know this Ronnie, it's like Dude 101." Shane points at his stomach. "In here is an unlimited capacity for food. It defies all known laws of physics and anatomy. It's the ninth wonder of the world."

"You boys never change," says Ronnie. "It's stupid the way you stuff yourselves silly."

"It's not stupid," I snap. "It's science."

Ronnie plants her hands on her hips. "Are you a dictionary now, or just a dick?"

I roll my eyes. "Don't you mean an encyclopedia?" I hike my thumb at Ronnie while still looking at Shane. "Why is she even here?"

"I just thought . . . ," mumbles Shane.

"Good job with that."

"Ollie—," starts Ronnie, but I cut her off.

"This isn't exactly how I want to spend my last day." Listen, here's the deal: Ronnie rocked my socks for the best week of my life, then she put my heart through a wood chipper. Do I still want her? Absolutely. Do I really want her around on my Deathday reminding me of what I lost? Not so much.

"Me neither," says Shane.

"You invited her."

Ronnie slams her hand down on the counter. "Fine. I'll leave then. Nice knowing you, Ollie. Good luck, I guess."

"Good luck? What the hell's that supposed to mean? I don't need luck to die. All I need is for you to stab me through the heart a few more times. Oh, hey! We're in the kitchen; let me get you a fork."

"Forget it."

"No forgetting it." My temples are pounding and my stomach is spewing acid into my throat. "You dumped me, remember? You don't get to be here and pretend like you're still my best friend and everything's all right."

Ronnie's face is pinker than normal and the little muscles in her jaw twitch like crazy. "I'm not the one who—"

"Jesus, can you both drop it?" Shane turns to Ronnie. "Try not to forget Ollie's dying." Then he turns to me. "How about you cut Ronnie some slack, man. She's here; she's trying. Do you really want to leave things like this?"

My own face, I'm sure, is as red as a cherry and my ears feel blistered. "Sorry if this death thing is a little hard for me."

Shane drops his pizza with a sickening slap. The warmed-over grease leaches into the cardboard. "And you think this isn't hard for me? I'm losing my best friend, dumbass. Tomorrow, when I want to tell you about something I saw on the Internet, I won't be able to. You can be mad at me and Ronnie and the whole stupid world if you want, but tomorrow you'll still be dead."

"You don't understand," I say.

Shane looks to Ronnie for help, but I know her well enough to see that she wants nothing more than to walk out of the house. "Fine," says Shane. "You're right. I don't understand. But if your big Deathday plan is to piss and moan and yell at your friends, then count me out."

"I just want *you* to be here."

Ronnie looks like she's about to snap but she takes a breath and says, "Ollie, what happened between us blew. I'll apologize if you want me to, I'll leave if you want me to, I'll spend the whole day letting you treat me like a punching bag, but I'm hoping that we can put everything behind us and go back to being friends. For today." Ronnie sticks out her hand.

"I don't know," I say. "It's hard—" Shane snorts and it's all I can do not to snicker. "You know what I mean." I stare into

Ronnie's eyes looking for something, anything, that'll help me, but she's harder to read than *Beowulf*. "Fine." I take her hand. "Friends. For today."

"Great," says Shane. "Now that there's peace in the Middle East, I'm going to enjoy every second that I have left with you." Shane does a drive-by grin and turns his attention to the pizza. "Let's start with this pie. So oily, so greasy." He picks up his slice, closes his eyes, and shoves as much of it in his mouth as he can. I won't lie; it's grossly impressive. "Ohh uud."

I pick up my own slice. The grease has already congealed into a squishy mess, but I take a bite anyway. I've had plenty of pizza before, but Shane's leftover pizza is the best I've ever eaten. The cheese is salty and creamy, and the marinara oozes down my throat. Shane peeks at me through his nearly closed eyes and smiles. We don't need to say anything. It's already said.

We eat in silence and, as much as I'm enjoying just being with my best friends, I'm sort of bored.

"What now?"

Shane busts out with a watery, gurgling burp that makes me a little nauseated. And also a little proud. "I'll be right back." Shane trots out of the kitchen leaving me and Ronnie alone.

"I'll miss you," Ronnie blurts out. She instantly realizes it's the worst thing she could have said. "Sorry."

"Don't worry about it." Silence. "My sisters cried, you know."

Ronnie laughs. "So you *can* get blood from an evil stone. Nice."

"Right?" Silence again. "I'll never forget the first time I met you. Third grade. Art. You were making a macaroni Death Star and I was rolling dried glue into boogers to fling into Mr. Alvarez's toupee."

Ronnie laughs so hard she snorts. "Oh, God, that was too funny. No one told him for like a week, not even the other teachers. He walked around school with glue boogers in his hair." We both laugh as the front door slams and I hear Shane coming back. Ronnie pushes her pizza away and sways from foot to foot.

Shane's got my backpack and a wicked grin. "Come with me if you want to—"

"Seriously," Ronnie says with a groan. "Is this really the right time for *Terminator* quotes?"

Shane gets scary serious. "Is there ever a wrong time for *Terminator* quotes?" Ronnie and I are silent. "Then follow me."

Curious, I leave to follow Shane, but as I'm about to pass Ronnie, she grabs my arm and says, "That wasn't the first time we met."

Before I can ask her what she means, Ronnie ducks around me and follows Shane.

"Hurry up, Travers!" yells Shane from his patio. "Stop wasting time!"

I tuck Ronnie's statement into my back pocket and trot out to the patio.

The Grimsleys' backyard is in worse shape than their living room. The grass is thigh high, and it's really more weeds than grass. There's a concrete island in front of the glass double doors, and in the middle of that island is a giant domed grill, into which Shane has dumped my books.

"What are you doing?" I ask as I join Shane and Ronnie

41

around the grill. All my books and worksheets and illegible notes flutter in the soft breeze. They're the sum total of all my high school knowledge.

Shane kicks the side of the grill and my biology book slides down to reveal my world history book and a motorcycle magazine that's more dog-eared than the *Hustler* I've got hidden in a Trivial Pursuit box at home.

"These are all your books," Shane says like he can't believe it. "I mean, at some point when you walked out of your house, you actually planned on spending your whole day in school."

I don't know why, but it's hard seeing my books sitting in the grill. Like witches on trial, I know they're gonna burn no matter what I say. "Where else did you think I was gonna go? It's kind of my life. I go to school, I hang with you, I chill at home."

Shane shakes his head. "Damn. You're in worse shape than I thought." Shane holds out a square tin of lighter fluid and a little silver lighter.

"What am I supposed to do with those?"

"Duh?" says Shane and looks from me to the books and back. "Burn them."

"But they're my books."

Ronnie suddenly grabs me by the shoulders, and I kind of wish she'd quit touching me so much. Listen, I'm harder than geometry 90 percent of my day already. With Ronnie around, I'm gonna hit critical mass. In my pants.

"Ollie," she says, looking me dead in the eyes. "You. Are. Going. To. D-I-E. You get that, right? You're worm food, frosty, a cold dead cadaver, buying the farm, toes up, living-challenged, www-dot-you're-dead-dot-com, tailgating with Jesus—"

"Yeah. I got it."

"You need to let go of all this. Your books, our fight—none of it matters."

Shane squeezes the lighter fluid onto the books until the thin stream is nothing but spray. The lighter fluid smells sweet, like sweat and sex. Or at least what I imagine sex smells like since there's a pretty huge chance I'm going to die a sad, lonely virgin. When he's done, he shoves the lighter into my hand and says, "Do it, dude."

"Go on, Ollie, burn 'em. You'll feel better."

The Zippo is warm in my hand. Heavy and solid, like I can use it to burn the whole world if I want to. And right now, I want to.

Whatever. I flick open the top and feel the potential fire, the flame that's about to be. The moment I turn the ridged, metal wheel I know it'll create a spark that will ignite the wick. For some reason that act scares me, you know? I mean, screw the books for a second. They belong to the school and, if I'm being honest, I don't really give a crap about burning school property. But burning them means I'm never gonna use them again.

I've dreamed about never having to go to school again, about throwing all my school shit out the window and hitchhiking to somewhere rad like Vegas or Idaho. It's just that in my fantasies, ditching my books was always the beginning of my story, not the end.

"Screw it." I strike the lighter and the fire springs to life like a pocket ninja. I turn my head and throw the lighter onto the books. Shane doesn't even flinch, which means that he's either got a stash of lighters just like it or that he's an exceptional friend. I'm going with door number two.

"Dude," says Shane as my books and the lighter fluid explode. I should say something poetic here, but "dude" says it all.

We stand back and watch the edges of my books brown and blacken. When my plastic binders catch, the fire flares green, which is cooler than free Internet porn.

My books spit up angry clouds of black smoke, like a signal to the school that they're in trouble.

"We should put these out," says Ronnie.

Shane goes to grab the lid but I say, "Wait."

"Come on, Ollie. Were you really that attached to your books?" He takes my shrug to mean that I can't put into words what I'm feeling about the loss of my books, but it's not the books at all.

"I'm sure they'll have plenty of books where you're going," tosses out Ronnie.

"I'm not sure how to take that."

Shane grins at us and says, "It works either way. If you end up in heaven—"

"Fat chance," says Ronnie, which earns her my superfrosty glare of doom.

"—I'm sure they'll have lots of books with naked girls in them for you. If you take a trip to the unhappiest place not on earth, chances are they'll have whole libraries filled with nothing but schoolbooks just like these. Only less crispy. Or more. I don't know."

The fire's a mess. It started out as a cotillion and turned into the dance floor at homecoming: hot and dirty and dark. I nod at Shane to put the top on and take a deep breath.

Everything feels new, it feels like my possibilities are endless. I get it. They were just books but they were also more than that. They were bonds that chained me to a world of school and homework and lame-ass rules. And now they're gone. Those rules no longer apply to me. I'm free.

"Let's get my day started. I'm up for everything."

I expect Shane and Ronnie to leap forward with some life-changing, orgasm-inducing plan that they've been holding in reserve for this exact moment. I figure the Amazing Plan is sealed in an envelope, like nuclear launch codes, just waiting for them to break that sucker open. Their blank faces tell me just how misguided I am.

"Come on, I'm ready. Better late than never. Let's raise some hell."

Ronnie serves Shane a look that's two parts confusion and one part constipation, and says, "Disney World?"

"Disney? Seriously? I'm not expecting crazy car chases and exploding buildings, but it's like you're not even trying."

Ronnie puts her arm around my shoulders. "It's your last day, Ollie. What do *you* want to do?"

"I don't know. I just . . . It's not like I spend all my time sitting in my room thinking about all the stuff I wanna do on my Deathday."

"Yeah, we know what you spend all your time in your room doing—"

Ronnie cuts Shane off. "Why don't we go inside and think about it? Maybe you can make a list of all the stuff you want to do."

"A list, Ronnie? That's so stupid."

"Shane? A little help?"

But Shane's already got a grin on. "No, he's right. It is stupid."

"Thank you," I say.

"It's stupid because we've already done it." Shane runs inside without bothering to explain.

The sun's beating down and I'm a freaking rotisserie in my hoodie. "Go inside?" Ronnie nods. I shrug her arm off and head in. Small streamers of smoke escape from the grill as I give my books one last nod.

"We'll figure something out, Ollie," says Ronnie when we're back in the kitchen.

I try to eat my pizza but there's something other than food and sex on my mind. "Ronnie, listen, if we're gonna be friends today, I gotta know something."

"What?"

"If you'd known I was gonna get my Deathday Letter, would you have broken up with me?"

Ronnie starts to answer and then stops. Her lips move but no sounds come out. Words, for the first time ever, have tunneled under the wall and escaped her. Finally, she just nods her head.

"Was I that bad of a boyfriend?"

"Ollie, please—"

"I just need to know." A crashplosion from Shane's room, followed by, "I'm all right!" distracts me momentarily.

Ronnie uses those few seconds to dam her tears. "Losing you this way is less painful than losing you the other way."

"Losing me what other way? You dumped me 'cause you thought you were gonna lose me?"

"It's more complicated than that. It's just—"

My anger rises like a thermometer in the Florida summer sun. "You never gave me a chance, Ronnie. You never gave me an explanation. You were my friend before you were my girlfriend, and I at least deserved that much."

Shane runs into the room, a little sweaty and a lot excited. "Okay," he says, "everybody pay attention to me."

We both look at Shane, who's holding some folded papers in his hand. He's about to tell us what they are, I think, when Ronnie busts out with, "I told you when we broke up, Ollie, that it wasn't your fault."

Shane groans. "Is *this* what you all have been doing? Should I call a shrink?"

Ronnie shakes her head. "No. We're good."

"For now," I add.

Shane waits to make sure neither of us has anything else to say. "Now, do you guys remember when Marvin Winkle died in the sixth grade?"

"Stung by a bee, right?" says Ronnie.

Shane nods but I can tell he's a little annoyed that she

interrupted. Again. "And do you remember how we each wrote out lists of the stuff we'd do if we ever got a Deathday Letter?"

I stare at the papers in Shane's hands. "Are those what I think they are?"

"Yes. Yes they are." Shane hands us each a folded piece of paper with our own name on the outside.

"I can't believe you kept these," says Ronnie.

I start unfolding mine. "Dude, am I really gonna want to spend the day doing stuff my sixth-grade self thought was cool?"

"This or Disney. Your choice."

"I'll take the list."

My cramped handwriting writhes on the creased page like I'd tortured it out of the pen. My handwriting has always been bad. Freshman year, my English teacher wrote at the top of the first and only handwritten paper of my high school career, *You're the reason God invented computers.* I couldn't argue.

"Well, Travers? What did twelve-year-old you want to do before you died?" Shane stares at me like he's gonna learn something from my list that he doesn't already know. I hate disappointing the kid, but he isn't kidding when he says he knows everything about me. It's minorly cool and majorly pathetic.

I clear my throat and read my list. "'One: be a *lucha libre* wrestler.'" Shane smiles and nods that I should keep going. He obviously thinks the first was a joke. "'Two: don't die. Three: see Mrs. Williamson naked. Four: grow a pornstache.'"

Shane snatches my list from me. "'Run through Tokyo in a Godzilla costume'?" He tosses the list in the pizza box. "What the hell is this, Ollie?"

"What?"

"Did you put anything serious on there?" Ronnie picks up the list and studies it. There's a ghostly oil stain on the main crease.

"I. Was. Twelve." I wait for Shane to stop looking at me the same way Mrs. Alley looks at me when I forget my homework. "I thought it was stupid. It's not like I'm allergic to bees. I always figured I'd die of old age in a diaper full of poop while flying cars drove by."

Ronnie folds the list and hands it back to me. "Somehow I don't think we're going to be able to 'learn the sacred art of the Samurai' before tomorrow morning."

"Well what have you guys got?"

Shane unfolds his list, adjusts his glasses, and clears his throat before reading. "'Swim with the dolphins, write a short story, jump off the East Indiantown Bridge, ride a motorcycle, jump out of an airplane, go into space, become president.'" Shane grins proudly.

"Great. I got it. You're awesome and I'm a loser." I pull a stool over and sit. "But I doubt we're gonna make it into space today unless you've got a rocket in your pocket I don't know about."

"What did you put on your list, Ronnie?" Shane says through clenched teeth.

Ronnie turns her list over and puts it down on the table. "Nothing. Nothing good."

"Come on," I say. "You have to tell me. I'm gonna be dead tomorrow. You can't resist a man's dying wish."

"You're not really a man," says Ronnie, "so I'm not sure you actually qualify."

Shane snatches the list out from under Ronnie's arm and holds it up. "'One: get boobs.'"

I laugh even though Ronnie just about pushes me over to get to Shane. "I'm *not* doing that," I say. "Unless I get to have Ronnie's boobs."

"Give it back, Grimsley." Ronnie's almost as tall as Shane, but he's quicker.

"'Two: build a rocket with Shane and Ollie.'" Shane stops and mock sighs. "Awww. I never knew you wanted to build rockets with us."

Ronnie stops jumping to get the list. "Duh! I played baseball, I swam in that nasty canal behind the Keesey house, and I even helped you freeze Ollie's underwear when he fell asleep first at our sleepovers. How could you guys *not* think I'd want to?"

"I never knew—," I start.

"Thank y—"

"—that you were so interested in our rockets."

Shane laughs so hard he almost lets Ronnie get her list back. "Good one, dude."

"What's next on her list?"

"'Make my mark on the world,'" says Ronnie. "That's what it says. 'I wanted to make my mark on the world.'"

I laugh again. "What's that even mean?"

Shane stops laughing and I don't know why until I see Ronnie's face. She's gone from being angry to desolate in the time it took me to make fun of her.

"Ronnie?" says Shane.

Ronnie leans on the counter. "It's what my mom told me the

day she got her letter. It was right before I moved here, before I met you guys. But before she died she made me promise not to squander my life. To be someone. That's what it means."

I'm stunned. We've never talked about Ronnie's mom. I mean, we know she died of cancer, but that's the extent of it.

"I feel like a total dick," I say.

Ronnie wipes the corners of her eyes and breathes out a smile. "No," she says, "this isn't about me. It's about you. About your day. Tell us what you want to do."

The problem is that I don't know. Obviously my list is crap, and Ronnie's list isn't much help either, except that she sort of got it right. I mean, what's my mark on the world gonna be? Who's gonna know that Oliver Travers was here? I think about my books, the freedom burning them gave me, and I get excited, but not in a hide-behind-a-bag kind of way.

I snatch up Shane's list and set it on the counter. I close my eyes and hold up my index finger like the pointer on a compass. Up and over and around I wave it until, finally, I drop it on the paper.

"Let's start here."

19:47

"Ollie, maybe this isn't the best idea."

"Can't you see I'm busy ignoring you?"

And I am. Ignoring him. Sort of. It's hard to ignore Shane Grimsley. He has a way of worming his way into everything that makes me want to give *him* a black eye. Currently, he's doing his pee-pee dance and trying not to look like he's going to barf on Ronnie.

I, on the other hand, am just being alive. You'll have to cut me some slack. Knocking on heaven's door tends to infect a guy with a little bit of sentimentality. But don't get too carried away, I'm not gonna run home and pop on *Grey's Anatomy* and bust out my hankie. What I *am* going to do is enjoy this view.

It's crazy how many times I've crossed the East Indiantown

Bridge. Just down the road is the best place in the world for hot dogs. Shane and Ronnie and I used to bike there all the time, especially on the weekends. We'd spend the day at the beach, pretending to drown each other and burying each other in the sand (Ronnie always built me boobs). Then we'd bike up to Hot Dog! for the best dogs on the East Coast. Loaded with onions and ketchup and relish and more mayo than God intended ever go on one foot-long piece of processed meat. Sorry, I think I drooled. Where was I? Right. I've crossed this bridge so many times and never taken the time to stand at the top and look out at the ocean and the sky and see how they flow into my town. It's like we're sitting right on the edge of the world.

There's nothing I can't see from up here. The boats on the ocean are smaller than the ships I used to play with in the tub. The Moriville Lighthouse, in the process of being restored (for, like, the last five years), is a sore red thumb poking high in the air. I can even see my dad's restaurant. Okay, I can see the brick wall and the Dumpsters on the side of the building, but still, I can see it. I wonder if Dad's actually at work. I mean, it's still too early for him to be there, but I wonder what he and Mom decided to do after I left. I feel a little bad that I'm not spending more time with them on my last day, but I know that if I'd stayed with them I wouldn't be standing at the top of a bridge getting ready to jump off. I'd probably still be sitting around the kitchen eating Return of the Living Eggs and avoiding my parents' hugs.

"It's fucking awesome up here!" I yell it as loud as I can, and a couple of fishermen way down the bridge stare at me like I just announced I was running for Miss America on a platform of peace on earth and puppies for everyone.

Ronnie slides her arm around my shoulders and I don't stop her. I do, however, get a little jiggly in the netherworld. "Nothing really matters up here, does it?"

"It's not the up here that bothers me," says Shane. He leans against the railing and gazes down into the water. "Just because Ronnie and I don't have letters doesn't mean this can't kill us. Or maim us. Ollie, I'm too pretty to maim."

I can't help laughing at Shane. There's really nothing the kid's afraid of except for heights. I've seen him pick up a rattlesnake with a pair of kitchen tongs. Hell, I've even seen the kid brave the Porta Potties at Moroso Raceway on chili dog day. But put the kid on anything taller than he is and he turns into a big blubbery mess. He's actually holding it together far better than I expected, but I suspect that has more to do with my impending date with death than increased intestinal fortitude.

I slip away from Ronnie and pat Shane's arm. "You don't have to do this," I say. "I'll understand."

"I won't," says Ronnie. "It was on *his* list. Grow a pair, Grimsley."

"Ouch, Shane. That sounds like a challenge."

"It sounds like it's easier to say I want to jump off the bridge while I'm sitting safe, at ground level, in my desk in sixth grade. That was years ago. This is now. And now is—" Shane peers over the side again. "Now is high."

"Then we'll meet you back at the car." I dance back and forth on my bare feet. All of us are stripped down to what we thought we could get away with. We're all barefooted. I ditched my hoodie and am left in jeans and a shirt so holey it could be pope. Shane had nothing to take off, so he's still in his same old shorts and T. And Ronnie. Well let's just say that God was smiling on me when Ronnie dressed this morning. All she's got on under her shirt is a white tank top and a black bra. A bra I'm actually pretty familiar with, if you know what I mean. If staring is a crime, I'm going to the gas chamber.

Shane looks like he's actually considering my offer, which I mostly didn't mean, when Ronnie grabs him by the front of his shirt. "Do you really want the last thing Ollie remembers about you to be that you wussed out on one of your own Deathday list items? How lame can you possibly be, Grimsley?"

I'm pretty floored. Ronnie's not usually the guilt-trip kind of girl. She isn't the kind of girl who makes fun of you for being afraid of animals that talk like people. Who forces you to watch *Finding Nemo* and *Chicken Run* and *The Lion King* even though they make you break out in a cold sweat and have nightmares for a month. Yeah, I'm talking to you, Mom.

No, Ronnie's usually not that girl, so I can't believe that she pulled that card on Shane. It's pretty low, pretty sneaky, pretty genius.

Shane slumps his shoulders and sighs. I can see it in his eyes: No matter what he says from this point on, he's committed. We might have to push him, but he'll jump.

Without waiting, I climb over the rail and lean forward. The water is calm and blue. I imagine floating on it and sailing all the way out to the ocean, the horizon, and right off the map. It occurs to me that this could be how I die. I know that I'm not gonna actually die until tomorrow morning, but I could drown and then be revived and end up on life support, with tubes breathing for me. Just an Ollie-shaped head of cabbage. Tomorrow morning could just be when my parents finally decide to yank the plug and put me out of my misery.

All my emotions surge through me as I contemplate the water. Fear squats in my feet, trying to claw its way up to my belly. Excitement rushes into me with every breath. I'm not just standing at the top of a bridge getting ready to jump, I'm taking my life into my own hands. Yeah, having a Deathday Letter is giving me more courage than I've ever had, but instead of waiting for Death to come and drive me away in a little yellow bus, I'm daring it to scoop me out of the water. And I'm dragging Shane and Ronnie along with me.

"Hey, guys?"

I look behind me. Ronnie and Shane are whispering. But they're arguing. They're whispguing. Argpering? Whatever.

"Guys!" Shane and Ronnie stop and turn. "What's going on?"

"Nothing," says Shane. "Right, Ronnie?"

Ronnie looks at Shane and then me. She starts to say something and then looks at Shane again before saying, "Right. We were just discussing whether we should jump from this side or the other."

"Definitely this side," adds Shane. "Now, what did you need, Ollie?"

There's something going on, something I can't quite figure out. They're acting like the time in fifth grade when Shane had to tell me that he was going away for the summer with his parents and wasn't going to be at day camp with Ronnie and me. I assume it has something do with my letter but the truth is that if I spend the rest of my day trying to sort out everyone's supergirly feelings, I'm never gonna get anything done. So I ignore it and move on.

"I'm not sure you guys should jump after all."

"What?" says Ronnie. Shane looks a little relieved but he tries to fake indignation.

I'm on one side of the rail and they're on the other. It feels like maybe that's how it's supposed to be. "I know I'm gonna croak. And it's possible that this is where it happens. I just don't want to be responsible for you guys getting hurt."

"Well good—," starts Shane, but Ronnie pushes him out of the way and climbs over the rail. She doesn't speak. She doesn't need to. Her brown eyes have gone all crazy. Shane sighs and follows her, caught in her gravity. And everyone knows you can't fight gravity. Or Ronnie.

"I'm not made of glass," says Ronnie. "If you're doing it, then so am I."

"Then let's do it."

"On the count of three?" asks Ronnie, and I nod. "Okay. One, two, three."

Nothing.

My arms are taut behind me. The muscles are stretched as long as they'll go and my fingers are anchored to the railing. Ronnie's looser than I am but she's wearing all her fear on her face. Shane is just a mess. He made it out onto the ledge, but now he's facing the road again, and he looks like he might cry.

"Hey, what're you kids doing?" yells one of the fishermen. We've also drawn the attention of the bridge attendant, who's up in his tower waving at us like he's trying to land a plane.

"Shane," I say. "We're running out of time here."

"Hey, if I'm going to do this, you're going to have to let me do it on my terms. How about you guys jump and I'll follow you down?" Shane crouches down and hugs the cement post. His whole body shakes.

Ronnie holds the railing with one hand. "Shane. Shane, look at me." Ronnie waits until Shane gives her his total attention. "I know this is scary, but it's fun too. And you're conquering your biggest fear. Just the fact that you're up here right now, on top of this bridge, dangling over the water, is pretty damn incredible."

Only that doesn't really help. Shane latches onto the railing tighter with every word.

The fishermen keep yelling but I tune them out. It's also a safe bet that the bridge dude in the tower has probably called the cops.

"Ronnie. Switch places with me." Ronnie nods and grabs the railing. I turn back toward the road and swing one of my legs around Ronnie so that I'm straddling her. My plan? Maybe not the best. Our faces are close. So close I can see the tiny little hairs in her nose move every time she breathes, and even her nose hair is hot. Not that nose hair is sexy. Just Ronnie's nose hair. She could be covered in nose hair and she'd still be sexy. If it wasn't for Shane's stifled whine, I'd be totally content to stay like this, looking into Ronnie's eyes, smelling her coconut lotion. But Shane needs me, so I move my other foot and let

Ronnie scoot sideways until she's on my left and Shane's on my right.

"Shane. Look at me, dude."

"Ollie." Shane's so scared he can barely talk.

"You can get down if you want, but remember what you said to me in the hall: We do everything together. We took a blood oath."

"Tabasco," Shane growls.

"It doesn't matter. What matters is that you're here. I'm gonna jump. I need to jump. I can do it alone, but I'd rather do it together." I hold my hand out to Shane.

"You know I'm right here, right?" says Ronnie, but I ignore her for now.

"Come on, Shane. Let's do this. Preferably before the cops get here."

Shane takes my hand with his, which is wetter than the river below us. Seriously, it's crazy wet. "You owe me, Ollie," he says through clenched teeth.

"I'll pay you back tomorrow." I wink at him. "First, let's get rid of these glasses."

"But—"

"If you can't see how high you are, maybe it won't be as scary." I pull my hand out of his and pull off his glasses before he has a chance to argue, fold them, and tuck them in his pocket.

"Oh, yeah. That makes it better," Shane says dryly. "You want to blindfold me too?"

"Guys?"

I look over at Ronnie. She points down the bridge where a couple of cars have parked and people are running toward us.

"On three?" I say. Shane and Ronnie both nod. "One, t—"

Shane leaps off the bridge with a scream. It isn't even remotely manly. It's the squeakiest, craziest scream I've ever heard come out of that boy's mouth. Even crazier than the time we watched all the *Nightmare on Elm Street* movies in one sitting and Ronnie taped chopsticks to her hand like razors and hid outside his window.

"Holy shit!" says Ronnie, and there's nothing I can say to top it. "I can't believe he did it."

The men behind us are yelling and more people are running toward us, but all I can focus on are Shane's flailing arms as he plummets. I lose my breath as I realize just how high up we are and how long that fall really is.

Then the splash.

Ronnie looks at me. She's excited. I can practically smell it. "You ready?"

I nod and take her hand. "On three?"

"Screw three."

"Jump!"

I won't lie. There's a part of me that's scared as hell. That part of me is buried in my gut, under layers of scary feelings about Ronnie. But it all goes away in the instant that I jump.

One second I'm holding Ronnie's hand, glued to solid ground, or at least a solid ledge, and the next second I'm suspended in the air and the rest of the world is nonexistent. Even Ronnie's gone. I don't know when I let go of her hand, but I

know that my hands are waving out at my sides, and I'm screaming out the last fifteen years of my life. I don't need my past
anymore because living in this one second is perfect. I forget
about dying and my parents and Ronnie and being dumped and
never seeing Shane again and how I never got to finish taking
the Little General to the firing range. All that's me is contained
in this one second.

And then it all speeds up. My stomach is in my throat and
the sky whizzes by me. The jagged air stings my eyes. The water
rushes up and for the first time I think that maybe we should
have waited until Shane had a chance to swim out of the way.
But it's too late. There's nothing I can do about it.

I'd piss my pants if I could but, really, all I can do is try to
straighten my arms and legs as I hit the water.

The crash into the water is probably what being sprayed
with a fire hose feels like. I don't even feel the wet—not right
away. All I feel is the need to breathe. I blew air out of my nose
as I hit so that water wouldn't go up my nose, and now I have
no air left.

Flailing like crazy, I scrape my way up. I don't even know
how far the surface is, I just know that I'm alive and I'm moving
and I need to breathe. But I can't get to the surface fast enough.

A hand takes mine and helps me up.

I break the surface of the water and slurp up all the air I can
handle, managing to drink about a gallon of water in the process.

The sun's bright, the water's warm, and I'm alive. Really
alive. And I realize the truth: I was dead yesterday, and I'll be
dead tomorrow, but today I'm alive.

"Huzzah!" I yell at the top of my lungs. Ronnie laughs some-where near me, and I hoot and holler at the tiny people at the top of the bridge.

"That was the coolest thing I've ever done," says Shane. I don't know where he came from, but he's on my right side and Ronnie's on my left, and we're laughing like we're insane. Which we pretty much are.

"Oh my God, I thought I was going to puke," says Ronnie.

"Thank you, guys." It's all I can say.

We bob up and down in the water for a minute, just basking in the fact that we jumped off the motherfucking East Indian-town Bridge. Pardon my language but, until you've done it, you just can't understand that there's no other way to describe it. I hereby rechristen it the MFEI Bridge.

"We should swim now," says Ronnie letting go of my hand.

I look at where she's pointing and see the crowd of people staring down at us. One of them is a cop.

Shane's not the best swimmer in the world, so it takes for-ever to get to the shore, but we finally crawl those last couple of feet and Shane kisses the sand.

"Oh, blessed ground, I'll never leave you again."

"I can't believe we just did that," I say, and howl again.

"I know!" Ronnie runs at me and I sweep her up in my arms, caught in a spray of adrenaline and emotion and . . . other stuff.

For the second time in less than an hour, I'm nose to nose with Ronnie, staring into her eyes. "I'm glad it was with you," she says. Her eyes flutter and start to close. Our lips are centimeters apart. I lean in and Shane yells, "We gotta run!"

I look over at Shane, ready to kill him, but he's pointing at a cop car coming down the service road. Its blue and white lights are strobin' freakylike.

Ronnie lets go before I have a chance to. She's embarrassed and I'm torn between scooping her up in my arms and leaving our past up on the top of that bridge or adjusting the rocket on the launch pad before it fires prematurely. I don't get the chance to do either because Shane and Ronnie both look to me to save them.

"We can't make the car," I say. "The cop will just run us down."

"Just show him your letter," says Shane. "He'll give you a pass, I'm sure."

I shake my head. "Hell no. Yeah, okay, maybe if I show the cop my letter, he'll let us go, but it would invalidate the whole experience. Jumping off the bridge is about more than challenging gravity, it's about challenging everything. It's about breaking the rules. If the cop gives us a pass, then we may as well have gone to see a movie."

"Then what?" asks Ronnie.

"There," I say. "We're making a run for it." I point at the old lighthouse. "Last one there buys lunch!" I dig my feet in and run.

19:16

Adrenaline floods my veins, completely replacing my blood. There isn't anything I can't do right now. The hill up to the lighthouse is crazy steep but I dig my toes into the grass and climb. I've never been able to run as fast as I'm running right now.

There's a buttload of historical stuff I can tell you about the Moriville Lighthouse. Or rather, there's a load of stuff I *could* tell you if I'd actually paid attention in fifth grade when we did a term on local history. But I didn't pay attention, so all I really know is that the lighthouse is old, it's been under renovation for years, and a lot of kids go there to do drugs. If you want to know the historical stuff, ask Shane.

I try to worry about what we're gonna do once we get

inside—let's face it, there aren't a lot of places to hide inside a lighthouse—but instead all I'm thinking about is how close I came to kissing Ronnie. It's not like we've never kissed before, we kissed a bunch of times during the week we dated, but this time felt different. Maybe because I'm different. Maybe jumping off the bridge made me a new man and her a new girl and we can forget our problems and go back to the ways things were before she broke up with me. She wants to; I know she does. I felt it in the air between our lips like static electricity.

Ronnie reaches the door first. Except it's not a door, it's a giant piece of plywood. It's graffitied with giant penises and lame tags like "Razer" and "Killbot"—the sort of crap only Moriville kids think is cool.

While catching my breath, I check down the hill.

"Looks like Tubby's gonna be a while," I say. Ronnie snorts and Shane takes a second to get some of the smeared water off his glasses. We're all wet. Soaked. Even the Florida sun can't bake us dry fast enough.

"Do you think he called for backup?" asks Shane.

I shrug. The Moriville cop shouts something at us as he chugs up the hill. I know it's a stereotype, the fat cop and all, but if the belly jiggles . . .

"What now, fearless leader?" asks Ronnie. She punches me in the arm and smiles.

Shane grins right along with her. Whatever they were arguing about on the bridge is forgotten. "I don't . . ." I look up at the lighthouse and something in my brain clicks. It's probably more of a *clunk* but you get the picture. "Come on, follow me."

I duck under the plywood and run inside.

The first thing I notice is the smell. Or smells. Plural. It's a fragrant mixture of wet raccoon, piss, and dust. And I can't outrun it. The whole place is permeated.

The second thing I notice about the inside of the lighthouse is that there's junk everywhere. Scaffolding and crates and even some stuff that looks like retail shelves. It's strange, like the inside is bigger than the outside. I know that it's not, that it's probably some engineering trick Shane could explain if I let him (which I won't), but it's still cool.

The third thing I notice is that, oh yeah, the stairs aren't finished. And that's kind of a problem.

"What's wrong?" asks Ronnie.

I point up. "We have to go up there."

"Up?" says Shane in a tiny voice.

"Come on then, guys," says Ronnie. "Unless Tubby has a coronary before he gets up the hill, we're running out of time."

I ignore Ronnie and grab Shane by the shoulders. "Shane. No thinking. We're going up to the top and I need to know right now if you can do it."

Shane contorts his face into a painful grimace. When I say painful, I mean painful for me. Seriously, the kid can do ugly when he sets his mind to it. "Ollie?"

"If you don't want to go, you can hide down here, but you have to make the decision right now and you have to commit. You can't whine and you can't back out midway."

"After the bridge," tosses in Ronnie, "this will be easier than Krista McMahon."

Shane chuckles and nods his head. "In."

"Awesome." I point to the scaffolding and say, "We have to climb that to get to the stairs." The concrete stairs built into the wall start about fifteen feet from the floor and go the rest of the way up.

"I'm out," says Shane.

Ronnie shoves him forward and says, "In is in. You can't pull out halfway."

Shane and I look at each other and giggle. Seriously. Giggle. The giggles bubble up from my toes like soda bubbles and pop out of my mouth. By the time Ronnie even realizes what she's said, Shane and I are nearly paralyzed. Then Ronnie's face turns crazy red and she grabs us both by our ears and drags us to the scaffolding.

"Ow!" I yell, but it's dotted with snorts and giggles.

Listen. No matter how old a dude gets, there are just certain things that can always make him giggle. "Doo-doo" is a given. "Duty" is another. Any word including the word "dick." "Benediction," "ridiculous," "contradiction," "dictator." Then there are random words, like "Bangkok" and "kumquat." And don't even get me started on phrases. I can't explain it. Guys are just hardwired for potty humor.

We reach the scaffolding at a stumbling laugh, but immediately begin climbing. Even Shane. I don't know if it's the laughing or if he's still floating on a cloud of freaky bridge-jumping adrenaline, but he tackles the scaffolding like he's king of the jungle gym. Hand over hand, he climbs right up, leaving Ronnie and me to scramble after.

I'm trying to concentrate on climbing, but Ronnie's ahead of me and all I can do is stare up at her. It's not like I want to be staring at her butt, but it's not like I can really help it either. And I'd be lying if I said I wasn't enjoying the view.

"Hurry up!" calls Shane. The cop still hasn't made it inside but Shane's all antsy.

Ronnie looks down and it seems like she's just now realizing that she's given me a front row seat to her ass. She climbs the last bit more quickly than even Shane and proceeds to give me the death stare for the rest of my climb, like I'd planned it. All I need is a black hat and big 'stache to twirl.

I try to apologize, but Ronnie edges past Shane and takes the steps two at a time.

Shane grins. "Dude, you are in *so* much trouble."

"But I didn't do anything."

"You really think that matters? Girl logic isn't rational, man." Shane pats my back and follows Ronnie up the steps. We're near the top when I hear the static of the cop's radio. I can't hear what he's saying, but I know he's in the building.

I put my finger to my lips and we keep tiptoeing up the steps. They dead-end at a doorless trapdoor opening, and we scurry through it.

"*Ollie, what—,*" starts Ronnie, but I cover her mouth with my hand and shake my head.

Getting down on my belly, I scoot across the dirty, dusty wood floor until my head is leaning out and down the trapdoor hole. Everything at the bottom looks darker. Possibly because the top of the lighthouse is so much brighter, what with the 360-degree view. Still, it makes it hard to see a fat cop in a blue suit wandering around among the shadows. If only I'd planned this out better, I could've laid out a trail of doughnuts leading into a cage and then shut the door behind him and made him dance. Dance, monkey, dance! Except, yeah, I didn't.

Someone taps my back but I shoo them away and keep watching for Tubby. Finally I see him by the exit. He looks around and then says something into his radio before leaving.

I heave a wicked sigh of relief and jump back up.

"We could have hidden down there," says Shane. His glasses magnify his eyes to the point that he looks like a freaky ventriloquist dummy.

I nod and say, "We could have. But then we wouldn't have been able to do this." I run up to the glass and look out over Moriville. There are still cars parked at the end of the bridge trying to find out what happened to us. Nosy old people who can't mind their own business. I can see everything from up here. My town looks so freaking small, but it's all I've ever known. I'm gonna die without ever knowing what it's like to live anywhere else.

Resolutely, I turn my back on my town. I put it behind me, drop my drawers, and press my skinny white ass against the glass. "Screw you, Moriville!" I scream, even though I know that no one can hear me.

Ronnie and Shane are both momentarily frozen, but I can count on my friends to join in, and they do. Even Ronnie. I don't look at her butt this time, and we *all* giggle.

"Promise me you guys will get outta here," I say as the giggles recede.

"Obviously," says Shane. "I don't plan on spending the whole day up in this musty old tower."

Ronnie groans and stares at Shane. "He means out of Moriville." She turns to me. "And yes, we promise."

"Good."

Right. Now things are awkward. Shane, Ronnie, and I are standing bent over, with our pants around our knees, our pressed hams out for everyone to see. Everyone possibly being my mom. I can picture it now. She's driving somewhere on some errand and she looks up and there's my white ass staring her in the face, burning out her retinas.

That doesn't happen though. Not that I know of. Instead, we hear a loud *thwack*.

"Someone's coming up!" Shane looks like he's gonna faint.

"Well, hide, dummy."

Shane bolts toward a door at the other end of the room and ducks inside.

"Where—?" begins Ronnie, but the huffing and puffing on the steps is enough to make us scatter. I spy a haphazard stack of boxes and grab Ronnie's hand. We barely dive behind them before Tubby's head pops up through the hole. How in the world he managed to climb the scaffolding, I'll never know.

Ronnie scoots as close to me as she can and we bury ourselves in the shadows of the boxes. It's not a great hiding place, and if our cop friend is even remotely thorough, he'll find us pretty easily.

Ronnie smells like the beach in the rain. Breathe it in long enough and there isn't a boy alive who wouldn't feel a little light-headed.

My anxiety rises when Ronnie squeezes my hand. Now I don't just have to worry about Officer Doughnut finding us and carting us away in the back of his cruiser, I have to worry about sweaty palms and my jack-in-the-box poppin' the weasel.

It feels like forever before the cop finally starts back down the stairs. I know he does because he curses as he hits his head going down. Ronnie grins at me and starts to get out from our hiding space. I shake my head and pull her back down.

"We should wait," I whisper into her ear, "until we're sure he's gone."

Ronnie nods.

Things are awkward again. I started my day not wanting her anywhere near me, then we almost kissed, now we're hiding behind some moldy boxes, practically horizontal. It's enough to make me crazy.

"Hey," I say. "What did you mean when you said third grade wasn't the first time we met?" I keep my voice as low as I can in case Tubby's just pretending to be gone. "You got here over the summer and started third grade with Shane and me."

Ronnie shakes her head. "I started at the end of second grade. One month before the end, to be precise. Dad moved us here after Mom . . ." Her voice is so close her lips nearly touch my ear.

"Can't be."

"Trust me."

"Okay, well just 'cause you were in school doesn't mean I met you."

Ronnie smiles a little, but it's not a real smile. "Oh, we met all right."

"Bull."

"It was my second day. No one talked to me much since I was the new girl. I ate by myself at lunch. I saw you and Shane, and I remember how much fun you guys were having. You didn't have any friends except each other but that didn't seem to bother you."

I stifle a laugh. "So you were stalking me and Shane, then?"

"No," says Ronnie. She almost looks like it's painful to remember. "I was watching you and then Shane pointed at me. You got up and I thought maybe you were going to invite me to come sit with you. I was so excited."

"Obviously I didn't ask. What happened?"

"You came to my table and asked me what flavor my pudding cup was. I told you it was chocolate. Then you took it and went back to your table."

"That's a lie. I never did that."

"I didn't talk to anyone the rest of the year."

"I'd remember that."

"It wasn't really that big a deal."

"We should go," I say. I stand up and pull her to her feet. "Wanna get Shane?"

I look for the cop car. It's gone.

"Ollie, you should see this."

Ronnie's standing in front of the door Shane ducked

through. I peek over her shoulder. Shane's sitting on the floor, his knees pulled up to his chest, dead asleep. All that's missing is his blankie. And don't let him lie to you, he totally has one. It's blue and green and the thing is holier than his underwear.

"How sweet," says Ronnie.

"Sweet my ass." I crouch down next to Shane and put my mouth by his ear. "You're under arrest!" I yell as loud as I can, and then jump back.

Shane jumps straight up and bangs his head on the under-side of the shelf directly above him. It's so hard I hear the hol-low *thunk* of his head. It looks painful. It's also funny as hell.

It takes a minute for Shane to figure out what happened and his face goes from disoriented to pissed in five seconds. "You ass!" He rubs his head and steps out of the closet.

I wait to make sure he's okay before I say, "Shane, when was the first time Ronnie and I met?"

Shane glares at me and says, "Dude, you stole her pudding in the second grade. You said she smelled like lima beans. When we started third grade, you wanted to be friends. Now listen . . ."

Ronnie tilts her head to the side and gives me a great *I told you so* face.

"God! Why are you even friends with me then?"

"Ollie, drop the pudding. It doesn't matter. You were, like, seven."

"But still."

Ronnie grabs my shoulders and says, "It doesn't matter any-more."

The three of us stand around. Wet, quiet, a little bored.

"We should go," I finally say. "Before someone tows your car."

"Where to next, jackass?"

"What?"

Shane points at Ronnie and says, "She gets an apology for something you did eight years ago, and I get nothing for getting a concussion?"

"You don't have a concussion," says Ronnie.

"Whose side are you on?"

"I'm sorry, Shane," I say. "Better?"

Shane's lip pops out and he pouts, a sure sign he's all right. "No. But I guess we should go."

"We need dry clothes," I say. "And a little more fun."

"Plus," says Shane, "I could eat."

Ronnie starts laughing and doesn't stop until we're back at the car, but I can't shake the feeling that there's more to the pudding than Ronnie let on. She remembered it, so she's obviously thought about it. And if I forgot about something so important to her, then what else did I screw up that I don't know about? Maybe everything really is all my fault.

Now I just have to find a way to fix it.

17:44 . . . TICKTOCK

I refuse to die in wet clothes." My clothes aren't so much wet as they are sticky and salty and just a little bit ripe. My green hoodie is still wearable, but the day is now nut-roasting hot, which is pretty typical for Florida. Sitting in the Jumbo-Mart parking lot isn't helping either.

"We can go back to my house, man. I've got clothes you can wear." Shane's got one arm draped over Miss Piggy's steering wheel and the other wrapped around the duct-taped headrest.

Ronnie clears her throat. "And what about me? Do you have clothes I can wear?"

"Is your dad home?" I ask. Ronnie nods. "Then we're definitely not going there. In and out, guys. This'll only take a minute."

"That's what she said," says Ronnie.

"Oh, God. Please, not this again."

"That's what she said," say Shane and Ronnie at the same time, and then they both crack up laughing.

"At least I know you'll still be friends after I die." I start to crawl over Ronnie to get out of the car but she pushes me back.

"What's that supposed to mean?"

"Just what I said." Shane and Ronnie both look clueless. "You know how some groups of friends are only together because two of them are friends with the third person, and when that third person's not around, the other two drift apart? I'm just glad that's not going to happen to you two."

Shane's face bunches up defensively. "It's not like we hang out when you're not around."

"I didn't say that."

"Shane," says Ronnie, but Shane ignores her.

"We're only friends because of you, Ollie. I mean, Ronnie's cool and we have fun, but we don't sit around gossiping and giving each other pedicures."

"Smooth, Shane," says Ronnie. She grabs her purse and gets out of the car.

"Did I miss something?"

"No," says Shane. "It's not what you've missed, it's what you're going to miss."

"I don't understand."

Shane climbs out of the car. "Don't worry about it. Let's go get some clothes and get on with your day."

Things just went from confusing to bizarre. First Ronnie and I almost kiss. Then she tells me I stole her pudding, and even though she says she's not carrying some sort of grudge, I can't shake the feeling that it's like a brown stain on our friendship. And now Shane and Ronnie are acting weirder than normal. On top of my own impending death, it's almost more than I can handle. Luckily, Jumbo-Mart is like a crazy world of its own: a place where all your troubles are lost in the yellow haze of fluorescent lights and the smell of savings. And by "savings," I mean "cabbage."

"What now?" asks Shane as we loiter around the front doors, where a cheerful woman with a chronic wave greets everyone. Most people ignore her but the greeter soldiers on. In a really small way, I'm glad that I'll never get to fail in life. Not that being a glorified mannequin at a Jumbo-Mart is being a failure. It's just that right now, I'm all potential. According to my parents and teachers, there's nothing I can't do. Which means that, short of winning an Oscar or the Nobel Prize, everything I would have done from this point on would be betraying that potential. Even if I'd wound up being a lawyer or an astronaut, my past still would've been littered with the corpses of the things I *didn't* do.

"Ollie?"

I shake my head and return to badly lit reality. "Now we shop."

"I don't have any cash," says Shane.

"I got it covered," I say, and pat my pocket.

Weaving around the masses, we get to the clothes. There are two kinds of people who shop at the Jumbo-Mart in the middle of the day: old people (of which Florida has an abundance) and parents.

The old people wander around like they're doped up (which they probably are) and the parents wander around, oblivious to the fact that their children's screams are shattering my eardrums.

Usually it makes my stomach bunch up and my jaw clench like crazy, but today might be the last time I nearly run down an old person who abruptly stops to admire a rack filled with parachute-panties, and I wanna soak it up.

"I have to go to the restroom," says Ronnie as we wander around the racks.

"Alone?" says Shane.

"Not all girls need a support system to tinkle." Ronnie navigates her way through the racks, and I watch her until she's just a brown head bobbing in a sea of poly cotton.

Shane and I have spent considerable time and energy arguing about what girls do in the bathroom that requires them to go in packs. Shane's idea has something to do with quantum entanglement, but I think that maybe, like a guy's hunger, girls go to the can together 'cause of some instinct left over from the days when the shitter was way out in the middle of some prehistoric monster's hunting ground. Taking a leak wasn't just something you did, it was a blood sport, so you peed in a group and prayed that if a saber-toothed tiger showed up for a snack, he gobbled up the girl next to you. When I told Mom my theory, she said it sounded a lot like her sorority.

"How about this one?" Shane holds up a white shirt that says MENTAL HELP WANTED on it.

I shrug. "A truer shirt was never written."

"Douche."

"Probably."

Shopping doesn't appeal to me. Never has. My mom does most of my clothes shopping. She's pretty good at picking out things that I'll like. I'd shop for myself but the problem is that I usually don't know I like something until she brings it home. When I look at stuff on the racks, it all just looks the same.

"What do you think's going on with Ronnie?"

Shane stiffens and stares really hard at a yellow shirt. "I already told you."

"Yeah, I don't mean about you, though maybe we'll get back to that. I'm talking about me." I grab a pair of crazy plaid shorts and tuck them under my arm.

"Oh." Shane's shoulders relax and he turns around. The first thing he sees is the shorts. He grabs them and tosses them on a table. "No."

"But—"

Shane shakes his head and gives me his crazy eyes. "No." He waits until he's sure I've given up on them before continuing. "So what about you and Ronnie?"

"We almost kissed. After the bridge. What do you think? Have I got a chance?"

"Of what? Getting back together? The outlook is dim."

"What about maybe hooking up?"

Shane shoves a black shirt at me. "How are you so dense?"

"What?"

"Ollie," says Shane. "You could probably use your death to get Ronnie into the sack, but is that what you really want?"

I shrug. "What I want is to not die a virgin. Dude, just being around her is harder than conjugating Spanish verbs. My balls are blue. They're cerulean. They're—"

Shane holds up his hands in surrender. "Got it. The less I hear about your balls, the better."

"So what should I do?"

"Go ice the cake in the bathroom. I don't know. I just don't think guilt-tripping Ronnie into boinking you is the way you want to go out."

"Who's boinking who?"

Ronnie wanders toward us with an armful of clothes. She looks different and she catches me staring at her. "At least one of you could have told me my hair looked like I'd had it styled by a blind paraplegic."

"It looks fine," says Shane over his shoulder.

"I think it looks great," I say. "Really brown."

"Thanks?" Ronnie picks up the shorts Shane took away from me. "Who would wear these?" She shudders and tosses them down again. Shane turns to me and mouths, *I told you so.*

We duck into the fitting rooms to change.

"Damn!" yells Shane from the booth next to mine. "I forgot to get underwear. Ollie, where'd you get yours?"

"Who says I'm wearing any?"

"Gross!" That was Ronnie from the room on my other side.

I make sure to yank off all the tags and transfer the contents of my pockets before exiting. "Much better," I say, and stretch my arms over my head.

Shane comes out holding his damp clothes. "Where are your clothes?"

"I left them. Not like I'm gonna need them." I grab Shane's out of his hands and toss them back into the dressing room.

Ronnie walks out of the dressing room in a skirt so short it makes mini look like a Puritan frock. And her shirt is a skintight baby T with a chick on the front. If my jaw were bionic, it'd be on the floor right now.

I elbow Shane and whisper, "My balls just went to DEFCON Blue."

Shane groans. He probably rolled his eyes too, but I've got tunnel vision for Ronnie. Shoot, Shane could have stood on his head and done the funky chicken with the Jumbo-Mart greeter and I wouldn't know.

Ronnie snaps her fingers in front of my eyes and I jump. "Hey. I'm up here."

"Sorry," I mumble, but right now, Ronnie's eyes are the least interesting part of her.

"Ugh, I'm going to change."

I grab Ronnie's arm. "No! I'll stop. See? Looking into your eyes. Your brown eyes. Your angry, brown eyes. Why are your eyes so angry? Don't be angry at a dying man. That's, like, sacrilege."

Ronnie's lips move but no words make it out. Finally she stomps her foot and storms off through the racks. I should probably follow her but watching her leave is so much more enjoyable.

"Ollie."

"Shane?"

"Are we going after her?"

"Just a sec." Ronnie doesn't look back once. Okay. Maybe she does. It's not like I'm looking at her head. Either way, I wait until she rounds the corner and then I say, "Okay. Now we're good."

"Do you need a minute alone?"

"Probably not even that long."

Shane pats me on the back. "Not what I meant. But thanks for that visual. I'll probably never sleep again."

I wink at Shane. "Whatever. You probably dream about me. 'Oh, Ollie, you're the best. Oh, Ollie.'" I fake French-kiss my hand until I realize that Shane's not there anymore and two kids in a shopping cart are staring at me. And so is their mom.

"Rehearsing for a play." Then I run.

When I find Shane and Ronnie in the video game section they look like they're arguing again. They stop when they see me.

"Again?"

Ronnie hip-plants her hands, which gives me an opening to check out her legs, and says, "No, this time we're talking about you."

"What about me?"

"Just what a dick you are," says Shane.

"And this is news to you how?"

Ronnie's face goes from smiling to stern to smiling to stern in the space of a couple seconds before letting a laugh escape. "I guess it's not. Bet I can kick your ass at Guitar Hero."

I steal Shane's grin. "Loser buys second lunch."

Okay, so you probably don't expect someone who's got just a little more than half his life left to be in a Jumbo-Mart playing a game involving a plastic guitar and Guns N' Roses songs. But it's not about the game. It's about losing myself in something for a minute. About being able to shut my eyes and forget that I'm dying. About hearing Ronnie yell, "I own you, Travers. You're going down!" instead of the pain in my parents' voices as they sent me off to school. Maybe it's not what you'd choose, but it's thirty minutes that I don't have to talk about dying.

I could probably go on this way for the rest of the day except that Ronnie totally shreds the fake guitar and unlocks a secret song that's both creepy and annoyingly appropriate.

"'Stairway to Heaven'? Really?" Ronnie leans the guitar against the glass case and steps back. "I think I'm done."

I laugh. "It's cool. Play."

"I really think we should get going. We haven't paid for these—"

"And we're not going to, Shane."

Shane gives me the antigrin. "That's not on the list."

"We're so far off the list right now. Forget the list."

Ronnie drops her voice to a whisper. "But shoplifting?"

I lean back against the case and cross my arms over my chest. "It's not about stealing—I've got money—it's about being able to do whatever I want." Shane and Ronnie exchange matching *I don't get it* looks. "Hey, you guys started this when you made me burn my books. Tomorrow I'll be a corpsicle, which means today I can do anything I want. There are no rules, at least none that apply to me."

"Fine," says Shane. "Then let's go paper Principal Pickle's house. Or find out where we can rent a Godzilla costume."

Shaun David Hutchinson

"We can't get to Tokyo before tomorrow morning, Shane. Use your head."

"No," says Ronnie, "but we can run around in front of Kellie Chin's house. Her grandmother lives with them and she's from Tokyo. Or Hong Kong. Or Seoul. I don't know. You get the point."

Shane winks at me. "We can always snag my binoculars and go see if we can catch Mrs. Williamson sans clothes."

"First off, Shane, buddy, pal, she was hot when we were in fifth grade. She's ancient by now. Second, it's barely noon. Unless J. T. Elementary has instituted a new naked teaching policy, we'll probably have a long wait."

"Then what do you want to do?" Shane's frustrated. It's not like he's tough to read. His forehead's wrinkly and his hands are jammed into his pockets and he's staring at me like he can burn a hole through my chest and see my bloody, beating heart.

"I want to turn toward the exit, walk slowly and inconspicuously in its general direction, and then leave without paying for these clothes I'm freeballin' in."

Ronnie shuts her eyes and chuckles. "I could've done without the visual. But what about after that, Ollie? Are we going to go knock over a liquor store?"

I shake my head and they both look relieved. "It's too early for drinking. I was thinking a comic book store." When Shane starts looking crazier than normal, I hold up my hands. "Calm down, Grimsley. I was only mostly kidding about the comics. I can't read fast enough to make it worthwhile."

"I don't like it," says Shane.

84

"Shane, Ronnie? Come on. If we get caught, I'll take all the blame."

Ronnie looks at Shane and says, "Fine by me."

I'm giddy and I don't really know why. Shoplifting? It's stupid. The last time I shoplifted was in the fourth grade when I stole a blinking magnet from a dollar store. For three days I had crazy-ass nightmares about the manager, a skyscraper of a woman who always wore a brown yarn shawl over a white shirt, brown slacks, and sensible shoes. She chased me until she caught me and hot glued a magnet to *my* back and stuck me on her fridge. She used me to hold up a list of potential names for her cats.

After the third night, I went back to that dollar store and shopleft the magnet right back where I found it.

But this time there's no scary manager to give me nightmares, and even if there is, I won't be alive long enough to care.

"Let's get going."

To be honest, I kind of expect that the second we walk out the doors, alarms and buzzers are gonna go off and a steel cage is gonna fall from the ceiling and trap us. Only that doesn't happen. Shane and Ronnie breathe a sigh of relief when we get out of the store without being chased, but I'm actually a little disappointed. Not disappointed enough to ruin my day but disappointed enough to know that what I need is a real challenge.

"Guys," I say as we walk to Miss Piggy. "I have an idea and you'll be happy to know that it doesn't involve stealing."

"Anything you want, Ollie," says Ronnie with a shy smile.

"I'm in," Shane says stoically. "So long as I don't have to climb anything else."

The fact that they both agree without hesitation says something important about Shane and Ronnie. It says what great friends they are. No. Scratch that. I mean, yeah, it does say that. But mostly it just says they're stupid.

I sling my arms around my best friends' shoulders and say, "Take me to The Velvet Underground."

The first time I heard about The Velvet Underground was during PE class in the fifth grade. Shane and I and most of the other kids who had already been tagged out in dodge ball were sitting against a wall in the shade when Manny Juarez showed us this flyer that he'd found in his father's bedroom. It was a poorly photocopied thing that showed an impossibly big-breasted woman straddling a floor-to-ceiling pole. Her legs were pointed into the air, her stilettoed feet forming the tops of the most erotic V known to man. She was gripping the pole with one hand while the rest of her body leaned back like she was comfortably reclining and didn't have a care in the world.

Underneath that was the name: THE VELVET UNDERGROUND.

It was like finding out that Shangri-la was real. There was even a phone number.

I burned that number into my brain, and later that weekend Shane and I called it. A woman answered and we were convinced that she was naked on the other end of the phone because we couldn't imagine a woman at a strip club having anything better to do than answer a telephone in the nude. Of course, we giggled and didn't say anything and after cursing at us, the woman on the other end of the phone hung up. But that moment was the first time we'd ever actually come close to a live nude woman.

As we grew up, other kids we knew would sometimes have stories about The Velvet Underground. Someone's dad would go to a bachelor party there or someone would drive by it. But it was always this mythical place that Shane and I dreamed about visiting one day.

I'd spent countless hours imagining a brightly lit building in the middle of golden fields, where women of every color and type and breast size imaginable stood outside waiting to welcome weary visitors into their sanctuary, where the men would be plied with alcohol and treated to lap dances and shows the likes of which I'd never be able to see over the Internet.

Some things should remain a dream.

"Are you sure this is the place?" I ask as we pull up to the off-pink building nestled between the railroad tracks and a check-cashing store.

Shane points to the sign and says, "Velvet Underground." There's hesitation in his voice. "I'm sure we can find a better strip club."

"Or how about we not find a strip club at all?" chimes in Ronnie from the backseat.

"No," I say, shaking my head. "We're doing this." I turn to Ronnie. "I know looking at naked chicks isn't your idea of a party, but we won't stay long."

Shane puts the car in park in front of the building but he leaves it running. "I'm with Ronnie on this one."

"How can you be with Ronnie? This has only been a dream of ours since fifth grade."

"Yeah," says Shane, "but look at this place."

I can't help admitting that the parking lot is definitely not a breeze-blown field of golden wheat. It's pockmarked like Danny Jackson's face, and it's littered with bottles of Boone's and cigarette butts.

"Maybe the inside will be better," I say with genuine hope. My thoughts go back to that blue flyer with the happy, limber woman on the pole.

"But probably not," says Shane.

Ronnie reaches over Shane's seat and puts her hand on his shoulder. "You know what? Why don't we just do this. If I can suffer through it, so can you. For Ollie."

I give Shane my crazy face and say, "Since when are mostly naked chicks who dance for dollar bills something you have to suffer through?"

Shane shakes his head. "That's not what she meant. I just don't think this is a good place. I heard about this place over off Forty-fifth Street that's probably cleaner."

"I'm going." I open the car door and get out without waiting for either of them to follow. With or without them, I'm gonna see some strippers.

Okay, let me just say for the record that it's not about the strippers. Okay. That's a lie. It is about the strippers. But it's also about doing shit that I wouldn't normally do. I'm not the guy who goes to strip clubs. Except that today I am. Today I'm the guy who jumps off bridges and runs from cops and steals clothes and looks at live naked chicks.

Because tomorrow I'll be the guy who's a corpse.

Now that I've gotten that off my chest, let's go look at some boobies.

The glass front door is tinted so dark that I don't know exactly what I'm walking into, which is a little scary. I look back and see Shane and Ronnie right behind me as I grab the handle and pull.

I walk in like I own the place. The inside is just as dark as the tint on the door. Maybe that's because it was sunny outside and in here there's barely enough light to see my hand in front of my face. But the second I hear the pulsing thump of the bass and see the swirly, patterned carpet, I know I'm right where I belong.

"Whoa, whoa, whoa," says a deep voice that echoes in my ears. I stop so short that Shane runs into my back and Ronnie runs into his. To the left is a booth with a grizzly man sitting inside. He's got a pencil behind his ear and his lip is swollen. Without wanting to know, I learn the reason for his bulging lip when he spits into a soda can. Brown juice dribbles down his lip and the side of the can.

"We're just here for the strippers," I say. Ronnie's choking behind me and I can practically feel Shane turning red.

"IDs." He looks back down at his partially completed Sudoku, like he's sure that we're going to turn and run.

"Sir, my name's Oliver."

The bouncer doesn't look up. "Does it say that on your ID, along with a birthday indicating that you're over twenty-one years of age?"

"That's just the thing, sir. If you'd just—"

"No ID, no entrance." He points at a giant sign on the wall that spells out the policy. Someone also wrote "No fat chicks" under it, but I'm pretty sure that's not part of the official policy.

I dig my letter out of the pocket of my stolen shorts and slam it down on the counter. "You know what this is?"

"Ollie, come on," says Ronnie.

"Unless it's your ID, you need to leave before I call the police."

Shane grabs my arm and pulls. "We don't need any more cops today."

But I'm not done. Some hairy, tobacco-chewing Neander-thal isn't going to keep me from seeing naked women. "That's a Deathday Letter. It means I'm going to die tomorrow. It also means that I can do whatever I want. And what I want is to sit at a table and drink soda and give some strippers a few damp and crumpled dollar bills. *Comprendo?*"

The bouncer looks up from his number puzzle and spits tobacco juice in the can. He doesn't even bother looking at my letter. "You should've tried a fake ID. Now, I don't care if you're going to stand in my hallway, douse yourself with gasoline, and light yourself on fire. Unless you're twenty-one and have an ID to prove it, you're not getting in here." He sneers at me. "*Comprendo?*"

I lunge at the window but Shane grabs the collar of my shirt, pulling me back so hard that it digs into my neck and chokes me.

"Screw you!" I shout so loud that my voice cracks. Shane and Ronnie drag me down the hall and out the door. The bouncer behind his little counter just laughs and laughs. "Asshole!" I yell at the top of my lungs.

Ronnie and Shane toss me out into the sun and I shove them off as soon as we're clear of the door. "Get off me."

Shane holds up his hands. "We're just trying to help, man."

"What was that all about, Ollie?" asks Ronnie. "We can try another strip club."

I cover my face with my hands to keep them from seeing me cry. "I don't want another strip club. I want this strip club."

"You don't want this strip club," says a voice over my shoulder that doesn't belong to either Ronnie or Shane. "The girls here are mean. And lazy."

"Who are you?" asks Shane.

I uncover my face and wipe my eyes and nose on my arm. I turn around and see a girl sitting on the hood of an ancient green Beetle. "Dru," she says. "I'm Dru."

Here's the thing about Dru: She's not pretty at all. Her nostrils are too big, cavernous really, and her eyes are sleepy, and her whole body is out of proportion, but she's so wrong she's right, like a bacon and banana sandwich. And the way she's sitting on the hood of her car looks vaguely dirty.

"Well, Dru," says Shane. "We're kind of having a private discussion here."

Dru smiles. "It actually sounds like the cute one with the black eye here was having a bit of a hissy fit."

"I was not—"

"Yeah," says Ronnie. "You kind of were."

"Well excuse me for dying."

Dru perks up. "You're dying?"

"I got the letter right here. . . . Oh, shit." I pat down my pockets and realize that the letter is still sitting on the counter inside the strip club. "I left it inside."

Ronnie sighs. "I'll get it." She turns around and goes back inside. Shane and I stand around awkwardly on account of neither of us really knows what to say to this crazy girl sitting on the hood of her antique car.

"So, are you a stripper here?" asks Shane.

"Didn't I say the girls here are dirty? Are you trying to imply that I'm dirty?"

I shake my head. "No, you called them mean and lazy."

"So then you're implying that I'm mean and lazy?"

Only Ronnie's return saves us from having to commit ritual suicide. She holds out my letter to me and I unfold it and show it to Dru. "See. Deathday Letter."

Dru grabs it from me and studies it. "Sad." She hands it back. "So your dying wish is to hang out inside The Velvet Underground? I mean there are better-looking girls working at Starbucks."

"Except that they don't take off their clothes," I say, and put my letter back in my pocket.

"Not always true," says Dru. "But that's neither here nor there. Calvin's a stickler. Without an ID you won't get inside. He wouldn't let his own mother in without an ID."

"Well, thanks for that information," says Ronnie. "But we actually have stuff to do."

"What kind of stuff?"

Ronnie looks to me and Shane for help but I got nothing.

"Yeah, what kind of stuff, Ronnie?" asks Shane.

"Well, I don't know. Stuff."

After watching Ronnie squirm long enough I say, "So why are you out here?"

"My sister's a bartender."

"Maybe she could—," I start to say, but Dru shakes her head.

"Not a chance. Remember what I said about Calvin? I'm not even allowed in." Dru fiddles with the hem of her shirt. "But I have some friends that might like to meet you."

Shane looks at her warily. "What kind of friends?"

Dru's loopy grin spreads across her face like butter. "The kind who might let you smoke some of their weed."

Shane shrugs at me, turns to the girl, and says, "You could be a cop or a kidnapper or something."

"What makes you think you're worth kidnapping?" asks Dru.

"I don't know," says Shane. "You could be trying to sell me into the sex-slave trade."

Dru nearly chokes on her laugh. "You caught me. So, do you want to come or not?"

"What do you think, guys?" I ask as we put our heads together. "It's obvious we're not getting in here."

Ronnie looks like she can go either way. "Could suck."

"Yeah."

"We could try a different strip club," says Shane.

"I don't know," I say. "This is the last time a stranger we just met in the parking lot of a strip club is gonna ask us back to her den of iniquity to get high and do who-knows-what else."

Dru cuts in with, "There probably won't be a 'what else,'" but I ignore her.

"It's your day," says Shane. Ronnie nods her head in agreement.

I break the huddle and say to Dru, "We're all in."

15:47

T his is the place?"

Shane, Ronnie, and I press our faces up against Miss Piggy's windows and stare at the mellow yellow monstrosity on the corner of Willow and 151st. "This can't be the place," I say. "And why are we here first?"

Shane sits back in his seat and looks in his rearview. "One, this was your idea. Two, the people who live here must be color-blind. Three, she's a stoner. It's not unlikely that Dru, if that's even her real name, got lost on the way to her own house."

Ronnie opens her door and I clench my teeth for the *screeee!* "We should go in."

"Without Dru?" I ask.

"Why not?" Ronnie gets out of the car and leans her head back in. "Dru said she'd meet us here and we are invited. Plus, Shane, I hate to be the one to tell you this, but your AC sucks balls."

"Speaking of sucking balls—"

"Sorry, Ollie, if it's not on your list, it's not happening."

I reach across the seat and punch Shane in the bicep. "Dude. Where's my list? And a pen?"

Ronnie snorts and laughs so hard she falls down in the grass. She stops laughing and gets up when she sees Shane hand me both items. "Guys, I was only kidding."

"Thirteen. Get my—"

"I was kidding!"

Shane spreads his hands and tries to look sympathetic, only sympathy isn't a naturally occurring emotion for the kid. "Balls are not a joking matter."

"Fourteen—"

"Ollie!"

"Jeez, Ronnie," I say, folding up the paper and tossing the pen back up front. "I was only playing. Can you not blow out my eardrums?" I crawl over the seat and stand with Ronnie.

"So I guess we're going in?" asks Shane, though it's really more of a statement than a question.

"How bad can it be?"

Of course, by asking that question, I'm guaranteeing that there's probably a giant, cleaver-wielding psycho behind that lime green door, ready to wear my skin to senior prom.

Knock, knock, knock . . . knock.

I hear no noise and begin to think that maybe this is all some gigantic joke.

Shane and Ronnie aren't even on the doorstep with me. They're both still spread out down the weedy footpath. It's a good strategy. If I do take a cleaver to the brain, they'll have plenty of time to scream like girls and run away while I'm dragged inside and hooked like a side of beef. My friends are the bestest.

The door's open a crack when I turn back around, the brassy security chain stretching from door to doorjamb. A blue eye and some blond hair are all I can see.

"*War ist das Kennwort?*"

"Do either of you . . . ?" I ask Ronnie and Shane over my shoulder, but the absolute lack of comprehension on their faces assures me that I'm not alone in my inability to understand what the heck the guy behind the door said. "Dude, I don't speak German. That *was* German, right?"

The blue eye blinks once. "Who are you little people?"

"We're high school sophomores, not escaped carnies," calls Shane. Of course, notice that he doesn't move any closer to the door.

"Shut up, Shane." I try to peek inside but the blue eye squints and the door starts to close. "Dru sent us," I manage to say. "I got a Deathday Letter and she said you had weed."

The door slams shut, leaving me to stare at the bubbling and peeling green paint.

Ronnie rests her hand on my shoulder and says, "We can find something else to do. I can call Troy Bissenger. He deals."

"Troy sells his kid brother's Adderall." I turn around to leave when I'm pulled backward and nearly lose my footing completely.

"Inside. Now. *Schnell! Schnell!*"

The door slams behind us before I'm able to reorient myself. I'm not sure whom I expected the blue eye to belong to, but it isn't a short, ripped dude with blond hippie hair and Shane's grin.

"I'm Klaus." He points at himself like he thinks we can't understand him. "Klaus." Then he turns and walks through a beaded curtain, leaving Shane, Ronnie, and me in near darkness.

The cramped foyer smells like feet. There are two exits other than the door, both strung up with bead curtains.

"Should we follow him?" asks Shane. He's practically hugging the door.

"I don't—"

Klaus walks back in, carrying a bag of Cheetos. "Letter." He holds out his orange-fingered hand.

I take out my letter. It's taken a beating but it's still brighter than any paper out there.

Klaus reads the letter and hands it back. "You don't work for the *government* do you?" His voice drops to a whisper for the word "government" and I suspect he might be an escaped mental patient.

Ronnie ignores Klaus and holds her nose. "So, wow, I think someone puked in here. Or is this just what hippies smell like?"

"*Klugscheißer.*"

"Should I be offended?" asks Ronnie.

Klaus shrugs and carries his bag of cheesy goodness through the other bead curtain. I follow without hesitation, led mostly by curiosity. Shane and Ronnie are right on my ass.

Klaus leads us into the living room. It's two parts lounge and three parts hippie harem. There's no couch, just a bunch of beanbag chairs and a battered recliner. There are blankets and stained pillows spread out everywhere. There's also a TV in the corner and the air smells of Sour Patch Kids.

"Wow," says Ronnie, pointing at the TV, which has Dave Matthews playing on it. "Way to be a cliché."

There are two guys and three girls sprawled out on the beanbags, one of whom is Dru.

"How'd you get here?" I ask.

Dru pushes herself up on her elbows. "Magic."

"Who are these lame-o's?" asks one of the boys. He's tall and lanky, with the brightest, orangest hair I've ever seen. Seriously, it's like fire sprouting up from his skull.

"I'm Oliver and my friends are Ronnie and Shane."

"What is this place?" asks Ronnie.

"Dru," says Klaus, "didn't you tell these *kiffer* who we were before inviting them over to share our drugs?" He wanders off to sit with the others.

An Asian girl with mean eyes but who's definitely not wearing a bra under her baby T sits up straight. "Seriously, Dru, how could you not tell them who we are?"

Dru chuckles and shakes her head. "He has a letter, Nariko, and he's kind of cute."

I start to giggle. Ronnie punches me in the back. "Someday

they'll come up with a cure for being a boy," she says under her breath.

"So then who are you guys?" asks Shane.

Dru points around the room. "I'm Dru. That's Nariko, Pete, Gay Pete, and Hurricane. Klaus is somewhere. We're all somewhere."

"I'm glad we didn't drive with her," Shane whispers in my ear.

"They're not our real names," says Nariko. "In case you're narcs."

"If they're not your real names," says Ronnie, "then why are you both Pete?"

The redhead is Pete and the guy on his other side is Gay Pete. Gay Pete reminds me a little bit of Regis Philbin for some reason and I keep waiting for him to ask me if it's my final answer.

"We both liked the name," says Gay Pete. "But you all can call me GP for short."

"I'm not short!" shouts Klaus.

Everyone ignores Klaus so I change the subject and move on. "So why do they call you Hurricane?" I ask.

Klaus snorts and crawls over to a green beanbag. "Because she blo—"

"How old *are* you kids?" asks Pete.

"Fifteen," I say. "Almost sixteen. Well he's already sixteen, but only barely."

"We're not kids," says Ronnie.

"Right," says GP. "Except that you are."

Hurricane smiles at me and I get my first good look at her.

She's not even remotely pretty. Nariko's drop-dead, and Dru's got her freaky so-wrong-it's-right thing going for her, but Hurricane is just this plain girl I wouldn't look at twice. The moment she opens her mouth though, I like her.

"Hello, pot?" says Hurricane. "This is the kettle calling. You're a fag."

GP rolls his eyes, sighs, and says, "Ha-ha. You're so funny. On a scale of one to hilarious, you're a bitch."

"Hey, I hate to be a pain," I say, "but can we just get high?"

Hurricane snorts so much like a pig I'm not 100 percent sure there isn't one in the room with us. "I like a boy who knows what he wants."

"Hurricane," says Dru. "You do know what jailbait is, right?"

Hurricane eyes me up and down. In spite of her not really being bone-worthy, Jangles does a little wiggle. "I'm nineteen, not Mary Kay Letourneau."

"Before we do anything, I want to know what this place is," says Ronnie. "Are you guys some kind of cult?"

Pete looks at GP. "Can you believe they have no idea who we are?"

"Scandal. We obviously need better PR."

Nariko takes my hand and pulls me down to an empty bean-bag. She motions for us all to sit. Then she joins her friends. "We're Citizens Uncovering Deathday Letter Evidence."

"Great," says Ronnie. "You're CUDDLE?"

They all nod and put on the same goofy grin.

"The Moriville Chapter," says GP proudly.

"Yeah," I say. "We're outta here."

"Aren't you the guys who believe Deathday Letters come from Martians?" asks Shane. I notice that neither he nor Ronnie have moved yet, so I relax. For now.

"Saturnians," corrects Dru.

"And that's only the one chapter out in New Mexico," says Pete. "We're much more enlightened."

"Is that why Dru invited me over here?" I ask. "It's not like I know anything."

Hurricane smiles at me and for a second it's like it's okay that I'm gonna die. "Every little bit of knowledge helps. Just knowing you helps us understand."

"I'm glad *you* understand," I say, "because I don't understand anything."

Ronnie takes hold of my hand and twines her fingers through mine. They're sweaty and kind of gross, which is comforting in a wet way. "Ollie, we're not here because they're CUDDLE. We're here because they have weed."

Shane barks out a laugh. He looks at me and then Ronnie, who's giving him major stink eye. "What?" he asks. "It's funny that you think the fact that these guys are potheads is somehow better than them being conspiracy nuts." Ronnie's still scowling at him. "Whatever. Bring on the drugs."

Klaus grins and crawls over the pillows to a wooden chest covered with horses. He opens the lid and pulls out a purple, flower-shaped vase with four tubes coming out of the top of the round base. "Medusa," he says, with the flourish of a shitty stage magician. "One hit and she'll turn you to stone."

Pete and GP and Hurricane clap their hands together like

it's show-and-tell and Klaus just pulled a giant Peruvian skull from his ass.

"Klaus," says Nariko. "Medusa's for special occasions only."

Klaus shrugs and drags the largish vase thing to the middle of the pillows. "*Beruhige dich*. This *is* as special occasion."

"Yeah," I say. "Death? Not so special. Sad and annoying, yes, but not special." I pull my hand out of Ronnie's. "What is that whatchamacallit?"

"It's a hookah, Ollie," says Ronnie.

I have no clue what a hookah is, but the fact that Ronnie does makes me feel like maybe I should too.

"Right," I say, nodding like I know what she's talking about. "A hookah. I knew that."

Shane sighs heavily, the same way he does whenever I veto his foreign language movie picks. Subtitles do not go well with Slurpees. "I'm out."

"What? Why? Dude, this is what we came here for."

"It's not that I don't want to, but I've seen this after-school special before. Someone needs to stay sober to drive. Since it's my car, I'll do it." I can't tell if Shane's relieved or disappointed.

Hurricane grabs my hand and pulls me over to sit beside her around Medusa. Klaus opens a small plastic container and pulls out a lumpy ball of weed. I know it's pot without even having to ask. It's dark and mossy with tiny red tendrils sprouting out of it. He puts it in a bowl on top of the hookah and spends a few seconds playing with it.

"You've been drunk before, right?" asks Hurricane. I nod

even though I've never really actually been the *Webster's Dictionary*'s definition of drunk. "Well, this is nothing like that."

"Okay," I say. "Then what's it like?"

GP shakes my shoulder and grins. "It's like . . . it's like . . . it's awesome."

"Wow," says Dru. "That's helpful."

"I got it," says Pete. "You change your own oil, right?"

"He doesn't even have his license yet," says Shane. He hovers on the edge of the giant circle of beanbags and pillows. Ronnie's between Shane and me.

Pete and GP laugh. "No," says GP. "He's asking if you, um, ever launch the hand shuttle."

"Whack off," says Hurricane. "He wants to know if you whack off." She rolls her eyes. "Will you boys ever grow up?"

There are things that guys do, right? Everyone knows guys do them. Guys can sometimes talk to other guys about them, but they're not something we sit around and have deep talks about. Shane and I have compared notes, but we don't chill at lunch going, "I got peanut butter and jelly, and last night I rubbed one out while *Gilmore Girls* reruns were on."

Girls are a different story. You don't ever talk to girls about that stuff. Not to them, not around them, not even in the same room with them. Ever. Which means when Hurricane starts asking me if I've ever medaled in the underwear gymnastics Olympics, I turn bright red and my ears start to burn. I look over my shoulder and Shane's staring at the ground like it's got the unified theory of everything written on it.

"I'll take that as a yes," says Pete, and continues without

pause. "So you know how there's that moment at the end where your whole body is relaxed and your eyes flutter like you could sleep and you feel like your skin could float right off? That's what getting high is like."

I look sheepishly at Hurricane. "Is it really like that?"

"I don't really have a penis, so I might not be the best person to ask, but it's like being in this other place where time's a little bit slower and your worries aren't really worries anymore."

I reach across and grab Ronnie's still-wet hand. "You in?"

Ronnie nods and scoots up on my other side. "After the bridge, this is cake." I can't decide whether she's trying to sound brave for herself or me.

"Hey!" says Shane suddenly. "Maybe this is what kills you."

Hurricane strokes my hair and I kind of feel like I should shake my back leg like a dog.

"No one's ever died from smoking pot," says Nariko. "Don't be a tool."

"Whatever," says Shane, and backs up farther. "I'll just be black in the corner over here."

Ronnie laughs. "Hello, welcome to Melodrama. My name is Shane Grimsley and I'll be your tour guide for the afternoon."

"Are we going to do this?" asks Klaus. "*Ich habe Hunger.*"

"Yeah," I say. "Let's do it." As soon as I say the words, my heart starts pounding and my shorts get less roomy and I can feel every single breath as I take it in and let it out.

"I'm ready," says Ronnie. She gives my hand a good squeeze and moves even closer. I suddenly realize I'm the filling in a Hurricane and Ronnie sandwich. I kind of wish I were sitting next to Dru or Nariko but I get the feeling that in a few minutes, girls will be the last thing on my mind . . . or at least not the first.

"That's four then," says Klaus. He sticks his tongue out at Pete and GP, who push themselves away from Medusa.

"All right," I say. "So what do I do?"

15:12 AND COUNTING

The smooth brass end of the tube is frosty in my hands and it bleeds into my fingers. It's pretty much all I can do to keep myself from shaking into tiny little bits.

"Just breathe in the smoke and hold it like you're underwater." Ronnie nibbles her bottom lip and tries to look like she knows what she's talking about. She should remember that I can always tell when she's talking out of her ass. Like right now.

"Last chance to back out and go to Disney, guys," says Shane from the corner. Honestly, I kind of forgot that he was there.

Here's the thing: Shane, Ronnie, and I never tried drugs. It's not like we were trying to make a statement or anything, it's just that we never did them. Never had the inclination to. My Deathday Letter sort of changed that. I have nothing to lose.

Which explains why I'm sitting around Medusa about to get silly, but not why Ronnie's here. Not that it's a big deal; it's just a little out of character for her.

"Ronnie," I say, nudging her in the ribs. "I get why I'm doing this, but why are you?"

"Because I want to be with you."

That should be the single hottest thing Ronnie—or any girl—has ever said to me. But there's this droopy knot of sadness in her voice. Sure, she's smiling at me, but her voice isn't. Her voice is sitting in a bathtub, listening to some tight pants–bad hair emo band, fondling a straight razor. And I get the feeling that I'm the cause.

Unfortunately, all the excitement has turned me into a quivering moron lacking the ability to form coherent sentences so all I can say is, "Cool."

"Hey," calls Shane. "If you morons get too messed up to walk, I won't carry you." Too bad I know he's lying.

"Right then," says Klaus. I realize that the CUDDLE kids are waiting on me. Not so patiently, either. "*Fangen wir an.*" Klaus gives us a tentative "all ready" sign, and I nod.

"Stick with me, kid, and you'll be all right," says Hurricane, and kisses my cheek. It's wet and I resist wiping it off with my shirt. "When he lights the top, suck on the tube. Not too much for your first time. Then hold the smoke in your lungs as long as you can before letting it go. Got it?"

I nod, even though I have absolutely zero clue what she means. Inhaling smoke is so counterintuitive. Like right-handed wanking.

Klaus sparks the cheapo green lighter over the top of Medusa, stares at the flame for a second, and plunges it into the weed. Hurricane, Klaus, and Ronnie all have their mouths on their tubes, and it's maybe five seconds (though it feels like a hundred years) before I realize I'm supposed to be doing the same thing.

I suck on the tube and I don't feel anything. I hear a sound like bubbles, only I'm not blowing them, I'm sucking them. Which doesn't make a tiny bit of sense. But before I can figure it all out, someone's stabbing me in the chest. With a white-hot knife they soaked in acid. Holy crap!

The tube's on the ground and I start coughing. Not just coughing, though. This ain't like I swallowed a sip of water wrong, it's like I swallowed a whole lake wrong. With all the boats in it.

Hurricane slaps my back a couple of times and Ronnie looks like she's torn between laughing at me and hugging me.

"Cap it off!" shouts Klaus.

The smoke is still stabbing my lungs, even as my coughing subsides. Hurricane hands me the tube and puts my thumb over it as she exhales a purplish cloud of smoke.

"You okay?" asks Ronnie. Her voice is strained with concern but her eyes flutter like she's about to fall asleep.

"Yeah," I manage to croak. Klaus and Hurricane aren't nearly as dopey-looking as Ronnie, but they're close.

"Ready?" asks Klaus. "It's easier the second time."

"Yeah," I croak again. It doesn't feel like it can get any easier, though. Thankfully, I no longer feel like my lungs are being

ice-picked by a stab-happy psycho, but I do feel like someone's opened up my chest, pulled apart my ribs, and sanded
them down.

Klaus lights the pot for the second time and this time I'm
ready with my tube. There's still some smoke in the hookah from
the last time, so the second I suck the bubbles, I feel it crawl
into my chest. I don't cough, but it's hard not to. Not because
this second time hurts, but because it feels like someone's in my
chest with a peacock feather tickling me from the inside.

Time stands still, and I feel the smoke inside my chest,
invading my cells with a box of Ding Dongs and a copy of *Pine-
apple Express*, and saying, "Who's ready to par-tay?" And yes, the
smoke says it *exactly* like that. Suck it.

As I blow out the smoke, it leaves behind this feeling of
weight loss, like I only weigh ten pounds and all my parts are
trying to fight gravity and lift off the ground. Which is totally
possible if I could just get some food. Damn, I'm hungry. Where
my stomach was just a few seconds ago is a micro black hole
that is going to devour anything and everything it can get its
grubby little hands on.

"Is this what being high feels like?" I whisper barely loud
enough for anyone to hear.

Hurricane snorts and laughs. I hear the others—Pete and GP
and Nariko and Dru—all laugh too, which makes me laugh. I
think.

"Don't make fun of the kid," says Klaus. "He asked a very
serious question and he deserves a very serious answer." Klaus
leans toward me but it feels like he's getting even farther away.

"Does it feel like you can do anything, anything at all, so long as you don't have to move?"

Hurricane snorts again, which I find both hilarious and hot. The only problem is that my go-go-gadget arm is off the clock. "Don't worry," she says. "You're high."

Ronnie shoves me and smiles. We both look at Shane, who's still sitting in the corner, but he seems like a mile away.

"*Wieder einmal?*" asks Klaus, and the funny thing is that I understand exactly what he said.

"Yes, please." Ronnie and I answer at the same time, and though I barely feel like I have the energy to laugh, I do have the energy to pick up the tube and take another hit.

Once the others get their turn, Klaus goes into the kitchen and returns with snacks, at which point Shane rejoins the group. Shane can't resist snacks. Especially not when the snacks are sour cream and onion chips, taquitos, salsa, soft-baked chocolate chip cookies, and loads of other bags filled with saturated fat and high-fructose goodness.

Everything tastes good, and I don't mean that in the usual way. It's like someone took all the chips and cookies and foods I've had a billion times before and sprinkled them with pure, unadulterated awesome.

Hurricane nudges me as I guide a bi-wing corn chip into my slack mouth. "How you feeling?"

"Orange."

Ronnie laughs and Shane groans.

"So what do you guys do, exactly?" asks Shane. "When you're not baked out of your minds, that is."

Pete swallows a handful of this and chases it with a cup of that. "We try to figure out why people like your buddy here get Deathday Letters."

Shane shakes his head. "What do you mean? People get a letter, and then they die. It's the way it's always been."

"Right," says Pete. "But who chooses who dies? Why your friend and not you?"

Dru stretches like an awkward cat. "See, we think it's a conspiracy."

Hurricane smiles at me, and for the first time I notice this ginormous Grand Canyon of a gap between her front teeth. "I personally think it's a population control thing. Some shady world organization selects certain people to die, sends them the letter, and then kills them off."

Ronnie and I both glance at Shane, who's barely controlling his desire to thumb his nose at us and say he told us so.

I'm trying to piece together some kind of argument but my brain's barely functioning so all I blurt out is, "That's stupid. People die every day."

"Six or seven thousand in the States alone," says GP. He's flat on his back, watching the ceiling fan spin around and around and around an—

Shane's the master debater and there's no way he's gonna let some stoners out-argue him. Which is lucky because, in my current state, I couldn't out-argue a can of tuna.

"Guys, the government doesn't know how people are going to die. They die from accidents and old age and disease. The government doesn't give people diseases or trip them down the stairs."

Dru sits up. Seriously, she's getting more catlike by the second. I'm just waiting for her to purr and sniff my butt. "Shane, can you be absolutely, one hundred percent sure?"

GP also sits up. He touches his wavy Regis hair like he's afraid it's moved in the last thirty seconds. Before Shane can answer Dru, GP says, "Here's a question for you. And I don't want you to answer, not right away. I want you to think about it. Really think about it. Then answer."

We all stare at GP until Pete backhands his knee. "Yo. Ask him the question."

GP shakes his head. I'm afraid the question might have fallen on the floor but he finds it and says, "Right. So here it is: Do people get their Deathday Letters because they're going to die, or do they die because they get their Deathday Letters?"

Shane starts to answer, and he's in full-on Exterminate! mode, but Klaus crumples his bag of chips and drowns Shane out, which is probably for the best.

"There are other considerations," Nariko says. "It's not all about conspiracies and aliens."

"Then what's it about?" asks Ronnie. There's genuine interest in her eyes. All four of them.

"For instance, if a prisoner on death row receives a Deathday Letter, should his final appeal be denied because of it?"

Shane finally manages to wedge a word in. A few words actually. "Um. Yeah. The Deathday Letter proves he's guilty."

GP sighs. "So young."

"All it proves," says Pete, "is that he dies the next day. His guilt or innocence isn't a factor, so his letter shouldn't be either."

"I don't get it," I say. The sad thing is that I didn't mean to say it, I was just thinking it and the words spilled out of my mouth. Mental note: Don't drool.

"Let me put it this way," says Dru. "No one really gets what Deathday Letters are all about. No one's ever tried to understand them. Everyone just accepts them as a fact of life, but what if we have some measure of control?"

"Still lost." Damn, didn't mean to say that either.

"Go back to the death row dude," says Pete. "He's on death row. He has an appeal. Then his letter comes, so the court automatically assumes that his appeal would have failed and they halt the process. The governor also takes it as a sign that he doesn't need to review the case. There will be no pardon. How can you be sure that the death row inmate didn't get his letter *because* the appeals process was going to be halted?"

Shane's eyes get big. Huge. Like, roll out of his head and bounce around on the floor gigantic. "You guys are talking about a causality loop. Do you even know what a causality loop is?"

Nariko raises her hand and says, "I have a B.S. from MIT. Klaus is in Mensa."

Ronnie looks at me and I look at Ronnie and we both say, "I don't know what a causality loop is." Then we laugh. Okay, more like we girlishly giggle. I wouldn't admit that if I weren't dying.

"They're trying to say that the prisoner receives the Deathday Letter, which causes his final appeal to fail, which causes him to receive a Deathday Letter. It's a loop. Or better yet, they're trying to say that the Deathday Letter isn't the cause of the final appeal failing, but rather that it's the effect, even though the letter comes before the failed appeal."

"Oh," I say. "Like how Ronnie broke up with me for being a jerk before I'd had a chance to be a jerk. Makes total sense."

Ronnie looks like I stabbed her in the back, but she doesn't say anything.

Shane tries to bury my comment by moving on as quickly as he possibly can. "Let's just say it's possible, which it isn't. It would change everything."

All the CUDDLE kids nod.

"*Du sprichst mir aus der Seele!*" Klaus throws his hands up in the air, causing a storm of chips to rain down on us. As I scramble to rescue a puffed cheese stick, Klaus goes on. "Even though they say they don't, doctors factor in whether a person's got a Deathday Letter or not. Why bother with a liver transplant if their letter says they die in twelve hours?"

"But you can't second-guess life," says Ronnie finally. "You can't stop a Deathday Letter, and even if you could, how do you know that trying isn't what leads to your death? Best just to use your time wisely."

"What about soldiers?" asks GP. "Men and women preparing to go into battle? They get up and go because they know they're going to die. Their commanding officers send them because they know they're going to die. What if they chose *not* to go to battle that day?"

"I don't know," says Ronnie. "Maybe a mortar shell blows up their barracks. That's the point."

"What do you guys think you can do about it?" I ask. My letter feels like a rock in my pocket. "Do you think you can stop people from dying?"

Hurricane strokes the back of my head. "No one can stop death, we just think that everyone should have the same chance to live."

Ronnie stands up. I look up at her, and she smiles and walks toward the kitchen. "Don't they?" I say.

"No," says Nariko. "That's what we're trying to tell you. Take you for example. Why do you have to die?"

I shrug. "Who knows? Maybe I have a tumor or maybe I fall down a well and Lassie's not around to help."

"And you act like you shouldn't even question it," says Dru. "What if you *do* have a brain tumor? Would you even try to have it removed?"

"I don't—"

"See?" says GP. "Most people don't know either. And even if they did, they'd have a hard time finding a doctor who'd bother."

"Some things are just better left alone," says Shane. "Not everyone needs to know the truth.

"Well, that's just stupid," says Ronnie.

I try to get a word in, but they've hijacked the conversation.

"Stupid?" asks Shane. "Who are you to say what someone should or shouldn't know? What if the truth just makes things worse? Did you ever think of that?"

"We're still talking about brain tumors, right?" says GP, but Ronnie keeps right on trucking over his words.

"Shitty truth is better than a lie." Ronnie seems like she's suddenly aware that we're all still here. "I'd rather know I had a brain tumor than die not knowing."

"Calm down," I say, but their voices keep rising.

"That's just you," shouts Shane. "Not everyone believes the same things."

"I bet Ollie would," says Ronnie. "You'd want to know, wouldn't you?"

"You don't have to answer that, Ollie."

"Guys!" I yell. Shane and Ronnie both hang their heads.

"What, Ollie?" says Ronnie. She looks at me through her lashes.

"What the hell is going on with you two?"

"Nothing," says Shane. "Just debating the finer points of Deathday Letters."

"Bullshit," I say. "You two have been bickering all day. And you think I haven't noticed, but I have. So tell me what's up. Now." Listen. I don't recommend using this tactic on your friends. Sometimes you have to treat a best friend like a yellow jacket you've got cupped in your hands. Give them time to figure shit out on their own. Of course, time is the one thing I don't have, so I know I'm pretty much begging to be stung.

"Just tell him," says Ronnie.

"Yeah," I say. "Tell me."

"Shut up, Ronnie. Just shut the hell up."

"Why don't you all just calm down; you're killing my buzz." Pete tries to stand up but he weebles and he wobbles and he falls flat on his ass.

"This isn't any of your business," I say.

"It's kind of our house," says Dru.

I stand up. I rise to my full height and I'm a giant towering over my friends, over everyone. It doesn't matter that this isn't our house or that we've pretty much commandeered the CUDDLE living room to have a linguistic slap fight. I just don't care.

"Now you both listen to me." I point at Shane and Ronnie with my index finger, shaking it like every teacher I've ever pissed off. "I want the truth."

"You can't handle—"

"GP," interrupts Hurricane. "So not the time."

"Sorry."

Shane crosses his arms over his chest. He's shut down. I've seen it before. I'll never get anything out of him now. "That's one thing you're not going to get. I don't care if you *are* dying."

Damn. That stings.

"Dude."

"Shane," says Ronnie, trying to touch him.

Shane pulls away. He fumbles for words before giving up and storming off to the kitchen. The beaded curtains rattle in his wake.

"I feel like I'm in a very special episode of *Gossip Girl*," says Dru. "The one where Blair smokes pot and acts like a dick to all her friends."

Nariko starts to push herself up, but GP grabs her wrist and says, "I got this one."

Hurricane tries to press one of Medusa's snakes into my fist, but I brush her off. "He's my best friend, Ronnie. You have to tell me what's up."

Ronnie shakes her head. "No, I don't."

"But you do know." It's not a question.

"It's Shane's secret to tell, not mine. I'll tell you anything else."

"Forget it. Don't do me any favors."

W ell, I'm hungry," says Pete. I wait for him to move because it's the only way I'm going to break this stupid standoff. I wish Ronnie would just cry already instead of looking at me like I stabbed her in the heart with a pencil.

Seconds drag by and no one's moving. Things aren't just awkward, they're painful. I finally look at Pete and say, "I thought you were gonna get some food?"

Pete rubs his belly and says, "I did. I went to the kitchen, made a peanut butter and jelly sandwich, and eated it. Then I came back and sat down. It was so fast you never saw it."

Hurricane high-fives him and says, "I wish I could move that fast." They've totally lost their stoner minds. They're absolute imbeciles—a bunch of stupid freaking asshats! And I'm trapped here with them in the most uncomfortable situation since the atomic wedgie incident of '03.

Ronnie scans the room like she's taking stock and trying to figure out how her day has gone so wrong. "I'm just going to go." She sounds so pathetic.

Dru has the nerve to look at me like I'm the Antichrist. In fact, everyone's looking at me like I just strangled a puppy and made it into a cap.

"Forget it," I say. "I'll go!"

The real problem here is that I don't know where to go. Shane went off into one room and I definitely don't wanna run into him right now, so I go through the only beaded door available to me. I think hippies like those beaded curtains instead of doors because no matter how mad you are, you can't slam them to make them sound angry.

The rest of the CUDDLE house is cluttered. The badly lit hallway is stacked with newspapers and magazines, and there isn't a single surface that isn't decorated with thrift store crap.

I go into the first bedroom with an open door. It looks like it was lifted straight out of a seventies porno (don't ask). The walls are wood paneled and the carpet is this puke green. There ain't much in the way of furniture: a faux wood dresser, a futon, a bookshelf. And the walls are plastered with posters of faraway places. Places I'll never get to see.

The futon's more comfortable than it looks. So comfortable that for a second, while I watch the dusty ceiling fan shimmy, I forget that I'm supposed to be mad at Ronnie and Shane.

I let my eyes go unfocused on a poster of a giant church in Budapest. I can almost imagine running fast enough to get there before I die. I feel the sun on my arms and the people bumping into me, cursing me in a language I don't know and haven't bothered to learn. In front of me is a crazy-ass church with spires that I think can almost reach heaven. If heaven really exists.

And I don't know if it does. I mean, what if it doesn't? What if tomorrow morning I die and that's it? No more Ollie. Ever. Everything I was ever gonna be is wasted. Every class I took, every book I read. I may as well have spent the last fifteen and nine-tenths years doodling my noodle and playing Halo. In the end it'll all amount to the same thing, right?

All this, this whole day, is pointless. Bridge-jumping and Ronnie and getting high. It's not gonna keep me from getting flushed.

"Hey."

Hurricane peeks her head into the room.

"Can you just leave? I wanna be alone."

Hurricane walks straight in like she owns the place. "This is my room, noob."

I look around the room again. "Really? I expected something more . . ."

"Girly?"

"I guess."

"I don't do girly." Hurricane goes over to her dresser and pulls something out of the top drawer. "I do do nunchucks, though."

She said *doo-doo*. I laugh even though I'm doing my best to stay pouty and depressed. "Cool."

Hurricane tosses the nunchucks on the bed and sits down beside me. "They'll forgive you, you know."

Sitting up on one elbow, I swear and say, "Forgive me? I'm not the one who needs to be forgiven. They're the ones keeping secrets from me."

"And you've never kept any secrets from your friends?"

"They're not my friends," I say, to avoid answering the question. I also try to avoid looking at Hurricane. Her blond hair is wavier, her blue eyes more blue. She looks so far away, but I can see every molecule. They look like doughnuts and I just want to eat her. That didn't come out right. Or did it? Damn pot. I can't tell if I'm hungry or horny or both.

Hurricane nods. "Really? Because if they weren't your friends, they probably would have given up on you after your first temper tantrum." She looks at me and scrunches her lips. "Oh, yeah, I'm assuming this is *not* your first episode."

"If they're really my friends, then they'd tell me what's going on."

"They *are* your friends, and your head must be really far up your ass to not know that."

"Then why won't they tell me what they're whispering about," I whine. Yeah, I whined. I think I'm allowed to indulge a little today. "Friends shouldn't keep secrets from one another."

Hurricane rolls her eyes and pushes me over. I fall to the side without trying to stop myself and then sit back up. "That's a load of hot donkey crap," says Hurricane. "And you know it."

"No it's not."

"Please. I'm sure you have things you've never told anyone. Not even your best buddy, Shane."

"No," I say. My jaw's getting sore from clenching it so hard, but every time I think about Shane and Ronnie whispering in the corner it makes me insane.

"You can't lie to me." Hurricane points to her eyes and then mine. "I see everything. I've got a little psychic in me."

"I don't care if you've got a whole psychic hotline in you. I'm not lying. Shane and I tell each other everything."

Hurricane scoots closer. "So what do you think this big secret is that they're keeping from you?"

I've been trying not to think about it. I tell myself it's because I'm too busy trying to have a crazy and wild Deathday, but the truth is that I'm afraid I already know.

"I think Shane's . . . that he's . . . I think Shane's been hooking up with Ronnie behind my back."

Hurricane snorts so loud I'm afraid she's going to choke on her tongue. "Wrong. That girl loves you. And Shane's your best friend. He'd never do that to you."

"Then why won't he tell me what's going on?"

"Come on, Oliver. Isn't there *anything* you've never told Shane?" Hurricane arches one eyebrow perfectly and stares down her crooked nose at me. It feels like she's looking at me through a fishbowl.

I sigh and slump my shoulders in defeat. "There may be one thing."

"See."

"But it's only 'cause it's really embarrassing. Like so embarrassing that if anyone ever finds out, I might spontaneously implode."

"Tell me."

I laugh. "If I've never told Shane, what makes you think I'm gonna tell you?"

"It might be cathartic."

"Who?"

"Telling me your secret might make you feel better."

"I'm mad at my friends, not overburdened by secrets."

Hurricane licks her lips in slo-mo like in a bad eighties rock video. All she needs is a motorcycle, a leather jacket, and a lollipop.

"What have you got to lose?" she says. "You'll be dead tomorrow. It's time to start living today."

That's the kind of saying that would normally make me roll my eyes and think of a cheesy greeting card. But the weed worming around my veins and arteries somehow makes it less lame.

"Fine. But I'm only telling you so that you'll leave me the heck alone. Or not leave me alone, 'cause I don't want you to leave. I just want you to stop bugging me."

Hurricane leans in closer. Private Willy leaps to ATTEN-SHUN! Her face is almost touching mine. It's so close I can taste the sweet ambrosia of sour cream and onion chips, and chocolate-chip cookies.

"Confess your secrets to me."

For a second, I think she's gonna kiss me. I want her to kiss me. So I close my eyes and wait. And wait.

And wait.

When I open my eyes, Hurricane is staring at me. I'm not exactly sure how red I am, but I'm guessing somewhere between bloodred and violet.

"Must've fallen asleep," I say, and try to put the broom back in the closet.

"Right," Hurricane says with the straightest face I've ever seen.

"So, my deep dark secret," I say.

"Sure." Hurricane looks like she's barely holding it together. Like any second a miniature, less chubby version of herself is going to split her stomach, crawl out, and cackle like a psychotic Halloween witch.

"So, it's not a huge deal. I just never told Shane 'cause he'd go telling everyone and well, you'll understand once I tell you."

"Then tell me."

I shake my head like a bobblehead doll. "Anyway. Late one night I was zipper surfing."

Hurricane sighs and looks up at the ceiling. "Oh my God. Does everything with you boys have something to do with your johnsons?"

Jeez. It's like she just asked if the sky's blue. And the look I'm giving her says that the answer is unequivocally yes. "You know," I say, "the fact that I'm stoned out of my mind is the only reason I'm talking to you about this."

"Sorry," she says. Hurricane runs her hands through my hair and I swear on a Bible that her hands are electrified.

"Cool. So I'm abusing the usual suspect but I'm just not that into it." I can't take the chance that she misunderstood, so I say, "Don't get me wrong, I'm always into it, I just wasn't digging the entertainment."

"Which was?"

"My mom's Victoria's Secret catalogs."

"You know there are naked girls on the Internet, right?"

"Duh," I say. The funny thing is how utterly easy it is to talk to Hurricane. Nana's the only other person I've ever been able to talk to about this stuff, but those conversations were never like this. "My parents keep the computer in the family room, and I'm not too keen on having an audience that consists of my little sisters, my parents, or my grandmother."

"Got it."

"So I flipped on my TV and muted it, hoping to find something stimulating, when I came across some scrambled porn."

Hurricane looks at me like I'm maybe the most pathetic thing in the world. Like I'm one of those puppies about to be euthanized. "That's so sad," is all she says.

"I was like thirteen. And it's not sad, it's resourceful."

"No," she says. "It's sad."

"Whatever. So I was like, there's a nipple, there's a nipple, is that a lap flounder? It did matter 'cause Erhard von Schlongstein had become Erhard von Longschlongstein and I took him to town."

"I'm not sure who this is more embarrassing for," says Hurricane, laughing.

She's right. I should be embarrassed. I should be frothing at the mouth, hiding under the futon, embarrassed, but I'm not, and that's ten tons of cool. "Things were looking up, and Moses was getting pretty close to the promised land, but I needed something more to push me over the edge. So I turned up the volume."

"Uh-oh."

"Don't interrupt. I inched up the volume and got back to the game, but something was off. I turned up the volume a little more and I heard a dude. Well, that's not a big deal 'cause, unless you hit the lesbian lottery, there's always a dude involved. But I looked a little closer and realized that the nipples were a little smaller than normal. A little closer and I realized they were also a little hairier than usual. I turned up the volume a touch more, still sitting there gripping Ivan the Terrible, and I realized that there wasn't just one dude talking, but two."

Hurricane laughs so hard she leans backward and almost falls off the futon. "You were whacking off to scrambled gay porn and you didn't even know it?"

"Well it's not like I finished. I mean, of course I finished, but I turned off the TV the second I realized what I was watching. Okay, well not right that second. There was that whole moment of horror where I had to think back and make sure I didn't actually enjoy it. Then I turned it off and finished."

"And you never told Shane?" asks Hurricane, though her words are more laughter than actual words. Still, I know what she means.

I shrug like she should already know the answer. "I don't want him thinking I'm gay."

"Would that be the worst thing in the world?"

"Being gay or Shane thinking I'm gay?"

Hurricane gets a hold of herself and leans back. It looks like it's maybe the most comfortable position in the world, so I join her. "Listen, I got nothing against the gays, but high school is a war zone. Every day's a battle to not be the guy everyone else makes fun of. Being gay or people even thinking I were gay would be like loading the other guy's guns and painting a bull's-eye right on my ass."

"I get why you wouldn't tell anyone, then. Even your best friend."

"Yeah. It would be the end of my high school career. Well, now it doesn't matter, but you get it. And I'm not saying I am, by the way. Gay I mean. 'Cause I'm not. I heart boobs."

Hurricane strokes my thigh. Shivers run through my body like all her electricity is being drawn to my lightning rod.

"Tell me about the girls you've been with, Ollie."

I gulp. "Not a whole lot to tell. Well, I mean, there's stuff. It's not like I've never been with a girl before, 'cause I've been with loads of girls. Boatloads. Whole shipping yards full. But if you're asking if I've ever, like, *been* with a girl, then I've only kind of been with one. Like half of one."

"Half of a girl?" asks Hurricane. "Which half?"

"I don't mean like that." I'm stammering like I've got a mouthful of Novocain. My lips are just mud flaps on a truck heading nowhere. "There was this girl at camp and we almost sort of . . . you know." How lame am I? I just admitted to jerkin' it to a gay scrambler, but I can't say the word sex.

Hurricane teases my ear with her finger and she scoots her

body so close that we're practically Siamese twins. "Tell me."

"It's kind of embarrassing."

"More embarrassing than masturbating to gay porn?"

"Good point." I clear my throat and try to arrange myself so my Eiffel Tower isn't so obvious. "Like I said, it was at camp. There was this girl named Emma. Emma Frotz. It was two years ago. Usually Shane and I went to camp together, but that year his parents took him to Switzerland for some smart people convention, so I had to go alone. Emma was at the neighboring girls' camp."

"Get to the good stuff, Oliver."

I nod. "Yeah. Getting there." I lose my train of thought and stare into Hurricane's blue eyes. They're so calm and deep and, and, and . . . "Right. Story. Emma and I, we flirted back and forth whenever we could. I didn't think anything of it. Let's just say that I'm kind of shy when it comes to girls.

"On the last night, she sneaked to my bunk and asked me if I wanted to go skinny-dipping with her and some of the others. I was like, 'Duh!' so we went. It turned into a giant sausagefest. More boys than girls."

Hurricane snickers. "Usually is."

"So Emma and I sneaked off to this clearing and started fooling around. It was, um, intense."

"What happened?"

I cough and rub my eyes to cover the fact that I *really* ain't all that comfortable talking about this with her. I mean, I guess it's one thing to tell a not-hot hot girl about the time I jacked my beanstalk to a couple of dudes playing hide the salami, but it's another to tell her about my experience, or lack thereof, with other chicks.

But she's insistent. "Emma was pretty aggressive. Didn't talk much, just sort of led the way, like sex was some mountain she wanted to climb. Anyway, she was doing some stuff I'd rather not explain when something with more legs than any creature should have goes crawling across my chest. I screamed as loud as I've ever screamed in my entire life and then sort of sat up and leaned forward. Okay, I don't really know exactly how it happened, but our skulls collided and before I knew it there was blood running down my face."

Hurricane's trying hard, for the second time, to stifle a laugh. "I'm sorry, it's just so funny."

"I ended up with nine stitches. Right up by my hair." I pull back my mop and show her the thin white scar.

"Ouch," she says, and traces it with her finger. My hair stands up on end.

"And I guess I don't need to tell you that Emma wasn't all that enthused about finishing what she started with a dude gushing blood."

"So you're going to die a virgin?"

I nod. "It looks about like that."

"That's . . . sad."

I start to get up because I don't need some girl's pity, but Hurricane pushes me back to the bed and straddles me. "What?"

Hurricane leans over me. Her hair is a blond canopy. "If you could do anything, anything at all, what would you do?"

"Well, I'd go to Spain because I've really always wanted

to run with the bulls, and then I'd go to stuntman school because—"

"With a girl," says Hurricane, putting her finger to my lips. "If you could do anything with a girl, what would it be?"

My breath catches in my throat and I swear I'm not sure I'm ever gonna be able to breathe again. This might be what kills me. All the blood my body needs to survive is making a beeline for the Wang Expressway and there isn't enough left for anything else.

"I have a list," I manage to squeak out.

"I bet you do," she says, and before I know it, Hurricane pounces. She mashes her face into mine and tries to suck the life out of me like a B-movie alien, except not as cool, but I go with it anyway. Her nose-breath steams my upper lip as she shoves her tongue into my mouth. It tastes worse than it smells and reminds me of the time my mom tried to make me eat liver. I try to use my own tongue to shove hers back into her mouth, but that only makes her try harder. It's like I'm trying to use a wet noodle to plug a hole in a leaky ship.

I haven't got the heart to tell her that if she thinks this is kissing, she's been doing it all wrong. It's wetter than my old friend Joey Henderson's bulldog.

But suddenly none of that matters; she could be eating my face instead of bathing it and it wouldn't matter 'cause she's got her hands at my pants, and she ain't shy.

"Did you forget something this morning?"

"Deodorant?"

"Underwear."

I shake my head. "I'm living crazy today."

"Makes my job easier." Hurricane grabs my shirt, pulls it over my head, and kisses me even wetter than before. Her hands start doing things that Ronnie's hands *never* did. And Ronnie definitely never used her teeth.

I can't believe I'm thinking about Ronnie while I'm here with Hurricane. *With* Hurricane. In the biblical and/or pornographic sense of the word. Ronnie thoughts can't be here. But they are. Her face and her lips and how they felt when we were together.

"Stop!"

Hurricane tosses her hair back and looks at me, but I pull her back down. "I didn't mean you."

Why should I feel guilty that Hurricane's here and she's doing . . . holy crap! I can't believe she's doing that. But Ronnie just won't go away. It's like I can smell her coconut shampoo and even hear her voice going, "Oliver Travers!" but it's not her.

Except it is.

"Oliver Travers, what the hell are you doing?"

Hurricane rolls off of me, which I think makes everything worse. Ronnie stands in the doorway, which is conveniently open, with her arms crossed over her chest, looking very red.

"We were just talking!"

"Oh, I forgot that you usually talk with your shirt off and a perfect stranger's tongue in your mouth." She says it with an iciness that scares the bejesus out of me. Seriously, the General doesn't just retreat, he surrenders.

I grab for my shirt but half of it is under Hurricane and it won't come out. Finally I give up and stand. My shorts try to fall, but I grab and hold them with one hand.

"Okay, Ronnie, you win. This is exactly what you think it is."

"All you ever care about is where you can stick your Wiimote!" Ronnie yells, and just stands there. I can see her brain working, the wheels spinning like crazy, trying to think of the next thing to say, but there isn't a next thing.

"Ronnie," I say, but can you believe she doesn't even give me a chance to say something stupid before stomping out of the room? I mean, come on! "Dammit!"

Hurricane touches my back, but I shrug her off. "Why won't she just listen to me?"

"Because she's upset."

"But she dumped me. She almost kissed *me* on the bridge. What the hell does she want from me?"

Hurricane grabs my hand and turns me around. "You love her?" I nod. "Does she know?" I shrug. "Well if she does and she caught you in here with me, she's got a reason to be mad."

"But she brok—"

"I didn't say it was a rational reason." Hurricane shoves my shirt at me and looks like she's waiting for me to do something "You should go after her."

But I can't.

13:43

Ollie," says Hurricane. "You've got to go after her. This is the part in the movie where the screen splits and the boy and the girl both regret the things they said and that they didn't work it out right then. Do you really want to spend the rest of your day staring out a window into the rain listening to Peter Gabriel's 'In Your Eyes'?"

I button up my shorts and pull on my shirt. "You talk too much. But thanks for . . ." I look back at the bed. "That."

The truth is that I'm still not sure if she was gonna have sex with me or maul me. In a small way I'm grateful I don't have to find out. If she boinked the way she kissed, it's possible I could have drowned.

That's not what's important, though. Ronnie is what's

important. But I'm torn. I didn't want to bring Ronnie along today. And then I did, and then I *really* did. On top of that, I feel guilty but I'm not sure what I feel guilty about. The fact that I was about to naked tango with Hurricane or the fact that Ronnie saw us? If I go after her I could make things worse but if I don't I could make them worser.

I know the longer I let Ronnie stew, the angrier she's gonna get, so I man up and march out of the room, leaving Hurricane on the bed. I stop at the door and turn around. "Later," I say. Then I go back to the living room.

"*Lippenstift.*" Klaus points at me and laughs his way around the biggest BLT I've ever seen. "*Lippenstift!*"

"Where's Ronnie?" I ask. It's just Dru and Pete and Klaus, and none of them look like they could buy a clue with a map and a million dollars. Okay, so it's not like I'm doing too much better. My head still feels like it's stuffed with Silly Putty, but I know I don't look as bad as them.

I snap my fingers in front of them a few times. "Hello? Ronnie? Girl-shaped? Came here with me?"

"She left with Nariko," says GP from behind me. He brushes by me and flops on the floor next to Dru. "You got a little . . ." GP motions at his lips.

"*Lippenstift,*" says Klaus again, though this time his mouth is so full of lettuce that it sounds more like, "Eppethbbbt."

"What do you mean, she left with Nariko?"

Pete motions with his hands like he's signing. "She left house. With Nariko. In a car. Forever. Away."

"We're better off without her," says Shane. I don't know

when he showed up, but I'm glad he's here.

"Shane, about earlier—"

Shane shrugs and looks at his feet. "It's cool. Don't worry about it."

No matter what Shane's not telling me, I can't stay mad at the kid.

"So, Ronnie left?"

Shane nods. "She didn't talk to me or anything. Nariko came into the kitchen while I was talking to GP and said she was taking Ronnie home."

"Then that's where we should go."

"I know I don't know you really well," says GP as he packs the hookah again. "But I think you need to remember something: This day isn't all about you."

I turn a little to face him directly but I get headrush and nearly fall over. "I'm the one who got a letter," I say.

"Sure, but Ronnie, Shane, your other friends, and your family, they're the ones who have to go on living. Yeah, you'll die, but they're still going to be here. You might want to cut your people a little slack is all I'm saying."

"Got it," I say, but his words go in and right back out. "Shane? Can we?"

"Okay."

I look around the room again, feeling slightly nostalgic. This *is* where I got high and almost had sex. But the house feels so small now. It can't contain me.

"Thanks for everything, guys."

Dru jumps up, steadies herself on the wall, runs at me, and

throws her arms around me. I fall back hard but Shane's there to catch us both.

"You're a pretty okay kid," she says. "I kind of wish you weren't going to die."

"Kind of?"

"You didn't see Ronnie's face after she saw you and Hurricane."

I pat her back. "Well then I'm glad only a small part of you wants me dead." Dru lets go of me and stumbles back to the couch.

"*Auf Wiedersehen!*"

"You're a dick, kid," says Pete. "Ronnie could do better."

"Good talking to you, Shane," says GP.

Shane grabs my sleeve and drags me out the door.

I'm not really sure how long we were in the CUDDLE house, but the sun is still high and so am I. The heat is pretty overwhelming and I'm already sweating. I can see why those guys stay in the house so much. The world outside is so harsh. The light, the heat, the sounds of random lawnmowers. For a nanosecond, I actually consider going back in the house and sparking up Medusa again. There are worse ways I can imagine spending my last day.

Shane stops in front of Miss Piggy and leans against my door. "How you feeling?"

Duh! "Great, Shane."

"What happened?"

"Don't you know?"

"All I know is that Ronnie hates your guts and just wanted to go home."

I shove my hands in my pockets and lean next to Shane. "I was busy being annoyed at you and Ronnie. Hurricane came in. We talked about . . . well, that part's not important. Hurricane started kissing me—"

"Whoa!"

"More like, 'waugh,' but it was still cool." In hindsight I start to think that maybe Hurricane wasn't as bad a kisser as I remember, but yeah, she was. Seriously, she was like a car wash. "She started doing other stuff."

"Define 'other stuff.'"

I shrug. I used to always be able to tell Shane almost everything, but knowing he's hiding something from me makes me hesitate. "Let's just say that when Ronnie walked in on us, I was shirtless and Hurricane's hand was in my pants."

Shane makes a silent O with his lips that looks like an inner tube. "Well it makes sense that she's angry," he says when the shock wears off. "But I still think we're better off without her."

I want to tell Shane that I wouldn't have hooked up with Hurricane, and Ronnie wouldn't have left if he'd just told me what's going on, but I can't. I want Shane to want to tell me. After all, we've been friends since before birth. He should trust me. The same way that I trust him.

"I once beat off to scrambled gay porn but I didn't know it was gay at the time because the sound was down and it was scrambled and there were nipples and I didn't know and then I turned up the sound and it was all dudes all the time and I shut it off right away but I was still scared to tell you but now you know. So there."

Shane stares at me. He's gone beyond Whoa! His face is starting to resemble a Halloween mask I wore one year that was a combination of Quasimodo and the Toxic Avenger.

"Shane? Say something."

Finally Shane regains his ability to form words into mostly coherent sentences. And he says something I totally don't expect. "Do you want to drive?"

"Drive?"

"Yes. Drive." It's like he's decided to ignore the hugely embarrassing and reputation-destroying secret I just spilled on the sidewalk, which might actually be for the best.

"You want me to drive Miss Piggy?"

Shane digs the keys out of his pocket and tosses them at me. "I want you to stop thinking about Ronnie. This feels like the best way to do that."

"Okay." Afraid he's going to change his mind, I run around to the driver's side, open the door with a *screeee!* and jump inside. "It feels weird being on this side."

"Ditto that," says Shane as he climbs in.

I jam the key into the ignition and start to turn it but Shane reaches over and pulls the keys out. "Don't jump the gun there, dude."

"I've taken driver's ed. This isn't my first time behind the wheel of a car."

Shane dangles the keys in front of my nose and says, "But it's your first time behind the wheel of *my* car."

"Fine," I say. I pull out my phone and pretend to be checking the time. Shane gives me a sideways look and I say, "Oh? Sorry. I was just checking to make sure I had enough time left in my life to learn to drive the Shane Grimsley way."

"Funny. Just put on your seat belt." I comply superfast to avoid the wrath of Shane and then give him puppy dog eyes for my next set of instructions. "Ugh," he says, and shoves his keys back at me. "Just drive. And don't forget to clutch."

Like I told Shane, I've driven a car before. But that was only with Mr. Valetti, and he had a problem with sweat. And the driver's ed practice car didn't have AC. There was no way to look cool in a Ford Taurus with no AC and a passenger who reeked of stale cigarettes and mold and constantly directed me to "Ease 'er on. Ease 'er on now." Not exactly the stuff dreams are made of.

Shane's car ain't much better, what with its salmon exterior and crap-colored interior. But it has AC, even if it's crap. Plus, Shane's car has one thing the driver's ed car never had: Shane.

"Now, you grab the stick and kind of jam it into first. My stick's a little different. It sticks a little more than others, so you just have to be firm with it and give it a good shove." Pause. "Are you laughing at me?"

I wipe the tears out of my eyes and say, "Are we still talking about driving?"

Shane reaches for the keys again but I slap his hand away. "Then pay attention," he says.

"Scout's honor."

"You didn't last two days in the Scouts."

"How about I swear on my life?"

Shane rolls his eyes. "Because that's worth a lot. Just drive."

I don't know which annoys Shane more: me stalling over

and over again or me laughing like a maniac every time I do. It takes me ten minutes to get Miss Piggy out of first gear and another ten to get into third.

"Now you've got it," says Shane as I fight the stick into gear and pull onto an empty road.

"I don't think stick shifts are supposed to be this hard," I say. "You should get this looked at."

"Twenty minutes driving and you're an expert? Just drive, douche."

"Yes, sir."

Not that I'm not grateful to Shane for letting me drive, but driving thirty miles an hour down neighborhood streets alongside bikes that sometimes go faster isn't what I had in mind for my first real drive. Of course, I can't really tell Shane that 'cause the fact that he's letting me drive at all is like my second miracle of the day.

I'm totally a candidate for sainthood. Saint Ollie. I like the sound of that.

In some ways Shane's worse than Mr. Valetti. He doesn't sweat but the first time I pull up to a red light on a hill he freaks out. There aren't really any hills in Florida, so it's more like an incline. That Nana could jog up. Seriously, I've seen steeper handicap ramps.

"It's okay," says Shane. "Just ease off the clutch and the car will roll back a little. Accelerate and you'll be fine." Only Shane doesn't look fine. He looks like he's gonna hyperventilate. Or puke. Or both. Then the shit really hits the fan when another car pulls up behind us.

"The nerve," mutters Shane. "Do they need to be that close?"

"It's okay, Shane. Really."

"And what do they need a Hummer for anyway?" Shane rolls down his window, sticks his head out, and says, "Do you live in a war zone? Are you transporting soldiers? Then you don't need a giant Hummer!"

"Everyone needs a giant hummer," I say, but Shane's not paying attention to me.

Before I can stop him, Shane jumps out of the car. "Back up! Give the guy some room."

"Shane," I call. "Light's green. Shane?"

"—act like you own the road because you drive a giant gas-guzzling, earth-killing tank! BACK UP!"

We almost miss the green light but that nice young lady in the Hummer does back up for me. Not that I need it. I try to mouth *I'm sorry* in the rearview but the woman's looking at her phone and not at me. I get us out of there fast, unsure whether she's telling her friends about the crazy, bug-eyed geek screaming at her in the middle of the road, or calling the cops.

"I think you're ready for something a little faster," says Shane. Frankly, I'm surprised as hell but I don't argue. "Head over to Military."

Military is a long stretch of road with only a couple of lights. It's the closest I'm gonna get to being on the freeway without actually getting on the freeway. Shane's really putting a lot of trust in me and I hope I don't let him—oops, was that a stop sign?

"Turn right," says Shane through gritted teeth. Seriously, the kid's gonna crack a tooth if he's not careful.

I turn onto Military and gun it. I shove the pedal to the floor and Miss Piggy, as if sensing my slow march toward death, gives me everything she's got. It's not a lot but it's still pretty effing awesome. It's like I'm flying without a safety net. The road blurs under me and the sunny trees wave as I pass. This is driving. This is what it feels like to have total freedom. To know that you can go anywhere and do anything. This is what I'm gonna miss.

It's like the steering wheel is showing me my future. Showing me all the zany road trips Shane and I aren't gonna be able to take. We'll never drive three hours just because. We'll never go fishing down in the Keys. We'll never spend a summer washing dishes at a greasy diner in some shithole town because we didn't bring enough money to fix Miss Piggy when she breaks down, and end up bringing together an entire town through the power of song and friendship.

All we have is this.

We roll up to a red light. I'm wind-whipped and smiling. Shane's smiling. I think we're both faking it a little, though. I think Shane knows what we're losing out on too.

I start to feel like I don't want to drive anymore but Shane nudges me and motions out his window. Stopped next to us is a blue Toyota something or other. The driver's not bad. A cute Latina with these sparkly white shades on. She looks over at me and I detect a little smile. I sure wouldn't kick her out of bed, even with that mole.

My heart beats a little faster and I grip the steering wheel a little tighter. I wink at her as the light turns green.

I don't even wait to find out if she smiles or winks back. I put the pedal down. I shift Shane's stick like it's butter. First to second to third to fourth to fifth. Each time, Miss Piggy roars as I clutch and shift. She's feeling what I'm feeling, and it's spectacular.

I howl at the wind as it tangles my hair, and fly down the road like Speed Racer. It's the most free I've ever felt. Even more than when I burned my schoolbooks.

Until I see the cop.

And the cop's flashing lights.

Oh, shit.

"This is gonna be bad, isn't it?" I ask Shane, and try to slow down, but it's too late.

Shane glares at me like he doesn't have the words to describe how bad it's gonna be.

"Oh my God, am I still high?" As I slow down and pull to the side of the road, I try to look into the rearview mirror to check my eyes but they don't look any different to me. "I can't go to jail, I can't go to jail, I can't go to jail, I can't—"

The blue and red lights are hypnotic. Every time they flash, a different image of my parents appears in front of my eyes. What are they gonna say about their little boy ditching school and doing drugs and getting arrested for speeding? Maybe they're the ones who actually kill me. Like in some sort of *Twilight Zone* episode. If I hadn't gotten my letter, I wouldn't have skipped school and they wouldn't have taken turns strangling me. In another nightmare, my parents let my sisters eat my liver while riding their ponies. And in yet another vision, they simply leave me in jail where I'm shivved by a fat guy ironically named Tiny, for calling him a *puto*, which I only do because one of the other kids dares me two rolls of toilet paper to do it. TP is mad currency in the clink.

By the time the cop gets to my open window, all those scenarios are swirling around in my head so fast that I just start to sob. Please don't tell anyone.

"I'm so sorry. I didn't mean to be driving but I got this letter and it says I'm gonna die and I don't wanna die and Shane said I should ditch school and I didn't want to but I didn't have a choice and then Ronnie came and we burned my books and I got really high and almost had sex with a fat chick named Hurricane because she blows hard and she does blow but not in the way I was hopin' and then Shane let me drive 'cause Ronnie's mad at me and he thought it would cheer me up and I don't wanna go to jail."

The officer stands at the window, eyes like lasers, searing my skin off in tasty strips. Only I can't see his eyes 'cause of his shiny silver sunglasses. And he might be laughing, I'm not sure. But I think he is. Which is kind of annoying. Jail is no laughing matter. Unless it's a clown prison. No. Not even then.

"Sir?" I say with a whimper.

"Let me see your letter, son." His voice is gravelly and I can't help thinking about the cop from *Terminator 2* who goes on a psychotic, yet surprisingly emotionless, rampage.

I dig my letter out of my pocket as fast as I can, and hand it to him. He reads the letter over and looks at Shane. "Are you the Shane he babbled about?"

Shane nods. He hasn't said anything since I saw the cop and I'm afraid he's maybe gone catatonic, only catatonic people don't nod, so maybe he's just gone mute.

"Can I see both of your licenses?"

Shane moves faster than I've ever seen. He's got his license and insurance card out before I can even manage to mumble that I don't have a license. The cop just nods and looks over Shane's license.

"And how old are you?" the cop asks me.

"Fifteen," I say. "But I'm almost sixteen. I have a learner's permit but I don't have it with me 'cause I didn't think I'd be driving. I lose stuff sometimes so my mom keeps it in her purse. But I'll be sixteen in a couple of weeks. I would've been sixteen in a couple of weeks, which is why Shane let me drive. Because I'll never be sixteen."

The cop clucks his tongue sympathetically. "Sad," he says. "But I can't let you drive around without a license, letter or not. I'm sure you understand." The cop cocks his head to the side. "How'd you get the black eye?"

"There was this really hot mom," I start, but Shane smacks me on the back of my head.

"I did it," says Shane. "Got mad at him for dying."

The cop nods like it's perfectly normal for your best friend to sucker punch you on the day you find out you're gonna croak. "Looks pretty bad."

"He punches like a girl."

"Well," says the officer, "that may be, but you should prob-ably let him drive anyway." He opens the door for me to get out and flinches at the *screeee!*

"I'm really sorry, Officer Todd," says Shane. I didn't even notice his name badge.

"Just don't let your friend drive anymore. Got it?"

Shane crawls over the parking brake and into the driver's seat. "Absolutely, sir. Ollie will never drive again. I swear. On my mom's life. Promise."

"All right then," says Officer Todd. "Good luck, kid," he says directly to me, and heads back to his car.

I just stand there on the side of the road in front of Miss Piggy, watching Officer Todd drive away with his words bounc-ing around in my head like a game of Pong.

"Good luck?" I can't breathe. "First Ronnie, now him. Why do people keep wishing me luck? Is there something I don't know?" I feel like I'm gasping. I don't know if I am but it feels like it. It feels like every time I take a breath, someone's sucking the air right back out of me.

"It's just something people say." Shane's far away. He's on the other side of the planet. But his hand's on my back. "Are you okay?"

I try to suck in a great big breath but all I get is a snatch of one. "No! I'm not fucking okay! I'm dying. I'm dead. My best friend is keeping secrets from me and the girl I love hates my guts." *BREATHE!* I put my head between my knees and try to slow down, but my blood's racing like the Indy 500, and there ain't a yellow flag in the world that can slow it.

Shane's voice is nothing but bees. Bees underwater. Except that bees would drown underwater. Whatever. It's all just buzzing.

Shane dives in and pulls me to the surface.

"Maybe we should just go home."

I shake my head.

"Then what?"

"I gotta fix things with Ronnie."

"Ollie—"

"Don't do that. Don't try to talk me out of it. Help me for once."

Shane folds his arms over his chest and I think for a second that I've lost him, that I've pissed him off for the final time. But he surprises me. It does happen sometimes.

"You have to show her that sex isn't the only thing you think about. You have to show her that you care about her. That you listen to her."

And then it hits me. I catch my breath. I feel the sun. I'm standing in a halo of light and that light is the most brilliant idea ever conceived. I know how to win Ronnie back.

"Let's go," I tell Shane. "I know what I have to do."

This is an *awesome* plan."

"This is a terrible plan. Worse than the time you filled your mom's hot tub with blue food coloring."

"She got over that. Anyway, this is different. This plan is guaranteed to work."

Shane looks in the backseat and says, "Any plan that involves a car full of pudding cups is a bad plan."

It took a huge chunk of the money Dad gave me, but I bought every pudding cup in three grocery stores. They're in the backseat and the trunk and every little space they can fit. On the way here I almost crashed because one got wedged under the brake.

On the upside, I didn't stall once. Awesome, right?

"Just help me unload these, Shane." I get out in front of Ronnie's house and try to keep the door from *screeee*ing, which is a big fail.

Ronnie's house is a skinny, cookie-cutter mini-McMansion in one of those neighborhoods where the Home Owners Association dictates the colors of the houses and how high your hedges can be. You know the kind. They're like tiny pockets of fascism.

I don't know if she's actually home or not. I didn't call first because I didn't want to tip her off that something might or might not be going on. Her dad's not home, that much I know by the lack of his car in the driveway.

Shane gets out of Miss Piggy and faces me with a cup of pudding in each hand. "Ollie. This plan is ridiculous."

"For the last time, no it's not. It shows Ronnie that I pay attention to her. That I'm about more than just sex. That I'm sorry."

"Uh, no. This plan doesn't say that you're sorry you tried to hook up with another girl while Ronnie was in the next room crying her eyes out over you and your fast-approaching demise. All it says is that you're trying to overcompensate for something you did eight years ago that you don't even freaking remember."

"You don't know what you're talking about, dude. You've never had a girlfriend." I reach into the back and grab more pudding. "Now help me or shut up."

It's broiling outside as Shane and I get the pudding cups from the backseat and trunk, and pile them on Ronnie's front lawn. I wonder how long the pudding can survive in the heat? I mean, they're in their little individually sealed containers and everything, so they should probably be okay. Anyway, it's not like I'm expecting Ronnie to eat all this pudding. I mean, she could. But I don't think she will.

And Shane's wrong. This has to work. I haven't got another plan. It seemed so clear when I was standing on the side of the road with my head between my knees trying to keep from hyperventilating, but Shane's words are like tiny brain-eating worms in my ears. What if he's right? What if Ronnie doesn't get that I'm just trying to prove something to her. I'm not sure what I'm proving but I know that this, what I'm doing, proves something.

"That's a lot of pudding," I say at the pile. Shane just grunts. The kid's got sweat bleeding out of his pores, soaking into his stolen shirt.

I'm trying to think about what I'm gonna do once we get all the pudding unloaded. Maybe I'll write an apology on her front lawn. In pudding. You know, something like: *Ronnie, I'm really sorry about the pudding. Mostly for not remembering about the pudding incident until today when you told me about it in the lighthouse, which was a lot of fun. Not hearing about the pudding. That was actually kind of embarrassing. The lighthouse was fun. You know what I mean.* Or something else. I can't make up mind. I know I'll come up with something. My finger is actually in an open pudding cup when I hear a door slam followed by, "What on earth do you think you're doing?"

"*Oh shit*," whispers Shane, and he backs away from me. "I was just a silent partner in this fiasco," he calls out to Ronnie.

"Thanks a lot," I toss back in his direction.

"Oliver Aaron Travers. What? Why? How?"

"Maybe I should start?" Ronnie gives me a steely death glare, so I continue posthaste. "I'm not sorry I almost crossed thirteen—"

"And fourteen," calls Shane.

I nod. "And fourteen off my list. I am sorry you had to see it, though."

"So basically what you're telling me is that you're sorry you got caught?"

Now I'm sweating. I honestly believed that Ronnie would see the pudding cups and run out of her house happy to see me, happy to know that I'd remembered, and we could get back to having last day fun. Things are not going at all like I planned.

"When you say it like that, it sounds so douchey."

"That's because it is, you idiot! You tried to hook up with another girl."

"We're not a couple, Ronnie. You made that abundantly clear. This is *my* day. My. Last. Day. Is this how you want it to end?"

Ronnie's red. She's magma. She's a shaken, stoppered bottle of champagne. And I think I just popped her.

"Is this how I want it to end? Are you kidding me? I don't want it to end at all. When I thought about you and I and the future, I never once imagined it ending on my front lawn surrounded by pudding cups." She pauses. "I should have never come along today."

I reach out to take Ronnie's hand but she pulls away like I'm poison. "Then why did you?" I ask.

"Because you're my best friend, you moron."

I sit on Miss Piggy's hood and fold my arms over my chest. "Then I don't get it. You should be happy I almost got to do . . . Hurricane . . . before I died. Look at Shane. He's not mad. He even taught me how to drive stick."

Shane chokes in the background but I'm currently in full-on Ronnie mode.

"That'd be fine, Ollie, if I were just your friend. But there's more than that here."

"I'm lost."

"Duh." Ronnie sits beside me on the hood. Close enough that I think maybe she's going to forgive me, which means Plan Pudding is a success! "I came along today because I knew I'd regret not coming. But you're still the same boy I broke up with. Except you're not. I know that doesn't make sense, but there were so many little moments today. On the bridge, in the lighthouse, around the fire, where I thought maybe, finally, you'd gotten it. You'd grown up. Then I had to catch you on top of the first girl who looked at you sideways."

"To be fair," I say, "she was on top of me."

Shane groans.

"You validated my biggest fear, Ollie."

"What? That I like girls?"

"No. That if I didn't give it up, you'd hop on the first girl who would."

"I mean, I guess you're kinda right."

Ronnie gets up. She's on the defensive again. I know what I meant to say and the words I said were sort of right, but they didn't have the desired effect.

"No, Ronnie, listen to me." I stand up so that I can look into Ronnie's eyes. "Just 'cause I was trying to cross shit off my list with Hurricane doesn't mean I didn't want to cross it off with you."

That, apparently, is an even worse thing to say.

"I knew it," she says, and stares off over my shoulder like she's going over our whole week-long relationship and validating every bad thing she ever thought about me.

"Stop acting like sex is all I'm about."

Ronnie looks me in the eyes. "But it is, isn't it? Even this lame pudding plan is nothing more than an attempt to get my forgiveness so you can finish what you and Hurricane started."

"I thought it would be romantic."

"It's not romantic, Ollie, it's pathetic."

Like all food eventually does, Plan Pudding has turned to crap. I don't get it.

"Why are you being such a bitch?" I ask. I can practically hear Shane's jaw hit the ground, and Ronnie's ain't far behind. "Yeah, I wanna have sex before I die. I wanted to have it with you, but I knew you wouldn't give it up so I took the one opportunity I had. Because *I'm dying*. That's the only reason any of this happened today. Jesus, I don't get you. You won't sleep with me, but you don't want anyone else to either. So, even though I shouldn't feel bad for almost getting with another girl since, oh I don't know, *we're not dating*, I brought you all this pudding to show you that I listen to you and that I'm sorry."

"I don't even like pudding," says Ronnie, almost snarling.

"What do you want from me?" I yell. "Why are you so mad?"

Ronnie looks like she's gonna cry and I feel like a douche because I'm the one who's making her look that way. "If you don't know, Oliver, then I'm not going to tell you."

By the way, usually when a girl uses that pearl of freaking logic, it usually means she's the one who doesn't know.

"That's bull."

"I really do wish I'd never come along today," says Ronnie. "Then you could have died without me finding out what a jerk you really are. At least I could have had my memories."

"Ronnie?"

The tears are really going now, and Ronnie turns away from me. I reach out to grab her hand but she tears it away. "I'm calling the cops. Get this pudding off my lawn and get the hell out of here."

I can feel the tears building in my own eyes. Everything's falling apart. "If I leave," I say softly, "you'll never see me again." It's not a threat. Just a sad fact.

"Good." Ronnie slams the door behind her.

12:08 . . . HALFTIME

"Come on, Shane, let's just try a liquor store."

Shane holds the two-liter bottle up in front of my face. He's a little sweaty from crawling around under his bed. For a minute it looked like his bed was going to swallow him right up.

"No way, man."

"But with my letter—"

"With your letter, you *might* be able to convince someone to let you buy some booze, but can we just pretend for a second that you don't have your letter?"

I'm kind of relieved. The whole idea of trying to buy liquor makes me a little queasy. Almost as queasy as looking at what Shane's swirling around in that bottle of his.

"I've been sneaking this stuff out of my parents' liquor cabinet one pour at a time."

The liquor is greenish, kind of yellow, and a little blue. It mostly looks like finger paint gone wrong.

"What's in it?"

"A little bit of everything."

"Is it gonna taste good?" Which is a stupid question to ask. Nothing that looks like a head cold is gonna taste good.

Shane shakes his head, confirming my fear. "Probably not. But it'll do the trick." Shane pauses. "We can go do something else."

"I know." This isn't on either of our lists but it's probably the closest I'm ever gonna get to doing the normal teenage rebellion stuff. It's pretty much a two-man party in the woods behind Shane's house with a bottle of something vile, or nothing at all.

I take the bottle from Shane and unscrew the top. It smells like sweet buttery hell with a hint of mint. "Peppermint schnapps?"

"I guess," says Shane. "How'd you know?"

"Dad likes it. Says it reminds him of college."

"My dad doesn't have too many memories like that."

"That's 'cause your dad's a certified rocket scientist who probably spent all of college actually learning. Whereas my mom says my dad partied for two and a half years before dropping out and going to culinary school."

Shane and I head out to the woods. They're not really proper woods on account of everything in Moriville is mega-overdeveloped, but it's what we have. We built a fort out here in the scrub when we were like seven and called it the Bunker. It's not really a fort though, it's just some metal sheeting we found at a construction site and an old mattress that smells like wet dog.

"So what made your dad decide to bail on college and be a chef, anyway?" asks Shane as we walk. He pushes aside a palm frond that smacks me in the face. "Sorry."

"Mom said it was 'cause of a girl."

"Nice."

"Mom didn't think so," I say as I laugh. "It wasn't her."

"So, here we are." Shane drops the bottle and flops down on the mattress.

"Yup." I flip my phone and look at the time. "I got plenty of time before my parents will miss me."

"Don't worry, dude, they miss you already."

I pause and look at him funny. Funny like "Whaaa?" not funny like "Ha-ha." "You're not gonna cry, are you?" I ask him.

"Maybe a little at the end. I make no promises."

Dirt and dust and God knows what else flies into the air when I hit the mattress. I wriggle around and prop myself up next to Shane. "Don't worry, dude, the guy handbook says it's okay to cry when a friend or a dog dies. Since I'm your only friend, I give you permission to cry as much as your little heart desires." Shane smirks and I punch him in the shoulder. "Just not right this freaking second, ya big girl."

"Deal, Travers." Shane unscrews the bottle and hands it to me. "As the dying man, you get the first drink."

"You know, this—whatever it is—is probably what does me in."

"Just drink, wuss."

The concoction of every liquor from the Grimsleys' liquor cabinet doesn't smell any better in the Bunker than it did in Shane's house. In fact, I think the humidity actually makes it smell worse. And unfortunately, I've never encountered a food or drink that smells better than it tastes. However, since I'm not a pansy, I put my lips around the mouth of the bottle and tilt it back.

"No backwashing!"

The liquor burns going down my throat, and while it doesn't exactly taste like steamy, wet dog poop, it runs a pretty close second. Luckily, the peppermint pretty much overpowers everything else in the bottle, and I find that if I focus on that, then I'm okay. Well, not okay, but not dead either, and that's sort of the best I can hope for right now.

"That's terrible," I say, handing Shane the bottle. "I officially christen it the Grimsley Gut Punch."

Shane grins. Seriously, it's measurable in megawatts. "I have my own drink. That's so cool."

"I wouldn't get too excited. You haven't tried it yet."

"Down the hatch!" Shane gulps it without hesitation. I have to give him mad credit. If I'd seen the face I made after drinking it, I wouldn't have touched it with my worst enemy's lips. Add being the bravest person I know to the list of reasons why Shane's my best friend. Of course, that bravery doesn't stop him from almost spewing. He has to hold his hand over his mouth to keep it down and I, of course, laugh at him. "Holy crap! My drink tastes like a blended corpse!"

"You said it, not me." I begin to experience a warm feeling in my navel that slowly spreads like tentacles to my lungs and fingertips. I snatch the bottle away and take another swig before I lose my nerve. I shouldn't be surprised that it's worse the second time around. Maybe it's because I know what to expect or maybe because I let it linger on my tongue a fraction of a second longer than the first time, or maybe it's because whatever's in that bottle is a fermented potion of pure, unadulterated suck.

It does make me feel tingly, though.

Shane takes another drink, followed by another scary face, and leans back. "I can't feel my lips." He tries to make motorboat noises but just spits everywhere, making me laugh even more.

"Cool."

"Is this what pot was like?"

"Nah. This is different." I feel so worldly casually talking about pot and liquor.

Shane leans on his elbow and looks over at me. "How?"

"Just is." The words claw at my throat to get to the surface and I struggle to put them in order. "This is like being all warm in your covers on the coldest morning of winter when everything feels relaxed and right in the world. Being high felt like I was on Mars. And hungry."

Shane laughs so hard I'm afraid he might actually swallow his tongue. "That made no sense."

"It did before I said it."

"That doesn't make sense either." That makes us laugh even harder, though I'm not even sure why I'm laughing. I'm just glad I am. You know how there are all kinds of laughter, right?

There's the belly kind that makes your whole body shake and shiver and sometimes you forget why you're even laughing. And there's the kind of nervous laugh you make when you're afraid or when you've just ripped a stinky and you hope everyone will think it's the dog. And then there's the sarcastic kind of laugh you do to cover the fact that you're royally pissed. My favorite, though, is the kind of laugh that frees you. It's like your laughter is the key that unlocks the shackles of unhappiness. It's the kind of laughter that you don't question, you don't think about, you just let it carry you like a boat down the river. That kind of laugh is just what I need, right when I need it.

When the laughter finally fades, I take another drink and hand the bottle off to Shane. "You know. I'm kind of proud of you for not smoking."

"Thanks, Dad."

"I'm not joking."

"Don't make it a big deal. I just thought one of us should stay sober."

"Unlike now."

Shane shrugs. "We're within walking distance of my house. I'm pragmatic not a saint."

A loud belch tears outta my throat and damned near takes one of my lunches with it.

"Good one," says Shane.

"Thanks." It takes a couple of swallows before I'm okay enough to talk again without being afraid I'm gonna bring up some chunks. "Either way, you're awesome, man. You don't give a crap what anyone else thinks."

Shane rolls on his back and rests his hand on his belly. The air between us feels awkward, like maybe I crossed the line between sharing and scary.

"Ollie—"

"Shane—"

We both laugh and Shane says, "No, you go."

"What do you think dying's gonna be like?"

"Quick?" He looks at me and says, "Sorry. Wrong time for a joke."

"Seriously."

"Depends. We Grimsleys aren't big on the religion thing. If you can't use math to prove it then it's not really real."

"So you think I'm just gonna be . . . gone?"

"Don't know, dude. I hope not." Shane drinks some more punch. "I don't know about the God thing but it makes me feel better, somehow, thinking about you maybe hanging around, watching over me. Just not while I'm in the shower, okay?"

I chuckle. "Deal."

We let our words fade for a while, passing the bottle back and forth between us. The Grimsley Gut Punch starts tasting less like reheated ball cheese and more like scabby puss and fish heads, which, while slightly better, still sucks. I can't feel anything in my lips, and my fingers and toes feel like they belong to someone else. An alien maybe. I take off my shoes and socks just to make sure they aren't green or scaly.

"Seriously," says Shane. "You trying to make me hurl?"

"What?"

"Put your stinky-ass feet back in yo—," Shane starts to

say, but he's interrupted by maybe the loudest burp I've ever heard come out of that boy's mouth. It's so loud it sounds like a machine gun firing. *Rap, rap, rap, rap, gurgle.*

"Nice."

"I aim to please." Shane beats his chest with his fist to make sure it's all up. I'm laughing but when I look at him again, he's all serious. He's Captain Serious.

"Are you scared?" asks Shane.

The question blindsides me harder than Shane's sucker punch in the school hall. I mean, I know he's probably been thinking about it. And maybe he's just been waiting to get me liquored up enough to gush about it.

"I'm sorry," says Shane. "I didn't mean to ask. It's just that I'm scared of dying. Shit, I'm scared of living. I'm scared of everything that comes after every second."

"That's not true. You're a badass."

"Ollie, I'm generally scared of picking out what to wear to school. I'm not the badass. You are. You've been running around all day, jumping off bridges and stealing shit and making plays for any girl you can get your virgin hands on." Shane teeters like he might fall over, and he looks like he might fall asleep, but he takes another deep drink of his punch and barrels on. "So, I just have to know if you're scared and you're just doing a good job of hiding it, if you're too stupid to be scared, or if you've got titanium balls the size of watermelons."

I don't know how to respond and not 'cause I'm drunk. Even sober I wouldn't know what to say to that.

"None of the above?"

"Ollie—" says Shane, but I cut him off.

"Wait just a second for me to finish."

"You haven't really started."

"I will if you'll let me."

Shane mimes zipping his lips and throwing away the key.

"Better. The truth is that I'm doing my effin' best to ignore it. I'm pretending like I'm not gonna die, 'cause if I do . . . if I stop and think that this is my last day . . . if I stop and think about all the shit I ain't ever gonna get to . . . well there's a really good chance I might lose it."

"What?" Shane looks confused. And to be totally honest, the moment the words leave my mouth they leave my memory, so I pretty much have no idea what I just said.

"I'm not brave, Shane. I'm the opposite of brave. I'm that guy in dodgeball who hides behind the fat kid." I sit up and drool onto the bed. "I guess I just hope that if I do enough stuff, if I run fast enough and hard enough, I can outrun death. So yeah, I guess I'm scared. I'm a big freaking coward."

All three Shanes shake their heads. "You're not a coward, dude." I know he's holding something back, but every time I think I'm close to figuring it out I start to feel like I'm riding a roller coaster that's doing a double loop followed by a corkscrew.

"We would have had fun," says Shane. "Senior year."

"Senior girls."

"Prom and parties."

"Parties we wouldn't have been invited to."

Shane laughs. "We would've had our own parties."

The silence falls again. The funny thing about silence and best friends is that unlike, say, tequila, peppermint schnapps, and rum, they actually do mix. It's an awesome feeling to be around someone and know that every second doesn't have to be filled with talking. Sometimes just existing near each other is as cool as it needs to be.

The only thing that could possibly make this better is Ronnie's hand holding mine.

"What're you thinking?" asks Shane.

"That I hope heaven serves breakfast."

"Ollie, I'm being seriously serious."

"Serious. Got it." My head's swimming in punch. "I don't know. I was just sort of thinking about how you're my best friend." I decide not to tell him about missing Ronnie, too. It would probably just annoy him and I'm sure he already knows.

"Lame." Shane tries to sit up. It takes him a couple of tries. I'd help him but I'm laughing way too hard to help.

"Whaddaya want me to be thinking about?"

Shane rubs his temples. "Is there anything else you want to do before the big splat?"

"God, I hope I don't splat. I hope I die in a good way. I don't want it to hurt."

"Wouldn't it be funny if you drowned in a giant tub of pudding?" says Shane, laughing all crazy and hysterical. Drunk Shane is odd.

"Not funny, no."

"Oh God, it totally would!" Shane falls over and starts to

hyperventilate. Well, not really hyperventilate, but I kinda wish he would.

"Still not funny."

"I got it!" says Shane. He pulls himself up using the precariously placed beams of wood that hold up the metal sheeting. "Get up, Travers!"

"Stop shouting." I try to stand up but fall. And up, and fall. Finally Shane tries to help me but I manage to pull him down with me. We're all tangled arms and legs as we try to get back up. It's like a terrible scene from a Jim Carrey movie (just pick one, they all suck equally). Eventually we both get to our feet. We teeter back and forth, but we're standing.

Shane grabs my shoulders and says, "Listen."

"I'm listening but if I barf you're gonna be right in the cone of possibility."

"Then don't," says Shane, and backs off a little.

"Easier said than done," I say. Ugh. I hope my breath doesn't smell as rancid as Shane's.

"You're my bestest friend, Ollie."

"We've covered this. Do you need a hug? I can do a hug so long as no one's around."

Shane shoves me. "I don't need a hug. Yet. No. I think we should commiserate our friendship."

"I don't think that's the word—"

"Stop talking." Shane puts his index finger to my lips. Except that he sort of misses my lips and his finger kind of goes up my nose.

"Dude, trim your nails." The room's starting to spin and I pick a spot on Shane's forehead to focus on.

"Forget it."

Shane tries to turn around but I stop him, mostly 'cause he's the only thing keeping the room from turning into a Gravitron. "I'm kidding. Not about the nails. They're freaky long." I rub my nose. "Go on." Only I don't let him go on because I keep talking. "Doesn't the air feel pretty? Like the blue and the green and—"

"Let's get tattoos," blurts Shane. Then he pukes on my shoes, which makes *me* throw up. Luckily for Shane I'm able to turn to the right and avoid puking on his back.

It's fitting that Shane and I are drunk and sick together. However, let me just say that out of all the things I've done today, ralphing is the least fun. Less fun even than when Ronnie caught me getting biblical with Hurricane. Chunks of everything go into my nose. And FYI: Grimsley Gut Punch tastes about a hundred billion times worse on the way up.

"Tattoos?" I say as I hork up a big glob of mucous and bile and pizza. "Like the permanent kind?"

"Come on, it'll be fun." Shane looks like he's less drunk than I am. Maybe puking got some of it out of his system. "There's that place on Central. It's a like a four-mile walk. Besides, it's not like we have to get matching butterfly tattoos or anything."

"I do have to get home at some point. Family dinner," I say. Despite the fact that my stomach feels like a balloon poodle, the thought of food doesn't make me want to blow chunky soup everywhere.

Shane checks his phone. "I'll get you home in time. With your letter, they'll put us in right away. Probably give you a discount, too."

"Good," I say. "I spent most of my money on pudding."

"Ollie. You have nothing to lose. It's not like your parents can ground you."

I laugh. "Yeah, but they can kill me." There are a thousand reasons getting inked is a bad, bad idea, but I'm not ready for my adventure to end. No matter what, Shane's my best friend and if he wants to go get tattoos, then I'm on board.

"I'm in. But first I have to puke some more."

O AT is my copilot'?" I say as we stumble back to Shane's house. The last light from the day grasps at the clouds. "It looks like an ad for the stuff Nana takes to keep regular." By the way, what is it about old people and poop? Nana's always telling me to eat this or eat that so I'll have nice firm poop.

"That's fiber, not oat," says Shane, lowering his sleeve. "Your full name was too long."

I slap Shane's back. "It's the thought that counts, dude."

"Let me see yours again."

"You've seen it a hundred times," I say as I pull up my own sleeve to expose my skinny, pale arm. "It still says 'Carpe Mortediem!'"

"I know," says Shane. "I just want to find something wrong with yours."

"Good luck."

Getting inked didn't hurt as much as I thought it would. Meaning I didn't cry like a girl. I'm pretty sure Shane did though. Mostly it was just boring. I sat in a chair while a skinny giant dude named Karl talked about his hog. I know he was talking about his motorcycle but I kept imagining him on the back of a giant pig, racing down the interstate, picking up chicks.

There's something about getting inked with your best bud that bonds you. For the first time all day, I'm glad Ronnie isn't with us. It's not that I don't want to be with her and have everything be good again, but this is one thing between Shane and me that I'm glad I don't have to share.

"Hey, Shane?"

"Yeah."

"I'm sorry."

"They're your initials not mine."

"I'm not talking about the tat."

"I know."

"If you wanna have stuff that's just between you and Ronnie, then I respect that."

For the next few seconds it's just the shuffle of our feet. I don't know about Shane, but I'm so exhausted I could sleep for a week. Of course, my plan is to not sleep at all until I'm dead, but the four miles from the Bunker to the tat shop seems way longer on the way back.

"It's not that I like keeping secrets from you, Ollie."

I think back to my conversation with Hurricane. "It's cool, Shane. I ge—"

"Hypothetically, Ollie, if your best friend's keeping some-thing from you, it's probably because he's afraid you won't want to be his best friend once you find out."

"Hypothetically, that's bullshit. Hypothetically, my best friend could never do anything that would make me stop being his best friend."

Shane is quiet until we're close to his house. I can barely feel my legs, but if I listen closely enough I can hear them scream in agony.

"Hypothetically, maybe you know you'd never stop being his friend, and maybe he even knows it too, but that doesn't make it any less scary. It's hard keeping secrets, but it's even harder to tell them, especially if you're worried that telling will make the people around you stop loving you. Hypothetical best friends don't grow on trees."

As we stop in front of Shane's house, the puzzle pieces start to emerge from the fog of liquor and weed. There's just one thing I've ever kept secret from Shane because I was scared of what he'd think, and there's only one thing I can think of that he'd be afraid to tell me. Except I don't know how to go about asking him, so I just blurt it out.

"Shane, I know you're gay."

He's stunned. "How do you? Did Ronnie—"

"Ronnie didn't tell me anything. I figured it out all on my own. I'm not stupid, you know."

"How?"

"It's just that I finally realized we've been through every-thing together. I know everything about you, and there's only one thing I could think of that you'd be scared to tell me."

Shane kicks at the sidewalk. "And?"

"And what?"

"Do you hate me?"

"Don't make me punch you, idiot. Of course I don't hate you."

"I was so scared to tell you."

I clap Shane on the shoulder. "There's nothing you could do that would ever make me stop being your friend. Not even smokin' pole."

"Listen, Ollie. I don't even know if I'm . . . you know."

"Black? We've already covered this. You're definitely black."

Shane shoves me away. "Gay. I'm not sure if I'm gay. I think I am. I've been having some feelings."

"About me?"

"Hell no," says Shane with a laugh. "You're like my brother. And your 'fro's pretty tragic. There are blind guys with better fashion sense. And—"

"I get it, dude. Thanks."

Shane shrugs and concentrates on the ground again. "I didn't know what you'd think. It's so confusing. When you were being a major douche at the CUDDLE house, I talked to GP a little in the kitchen."

"Wait," I say, my eyes getting saucer huge. "You didn't?

Shane shakes his head. "No. I've never. Unless the Internet counts."

"Don't need the deets, Grimsley."

"I just don't know."

"And you don't have to. Gay, not gay, you'll always be my best friend."

"You're just saying that because you're dying." Shane gives me a halfhearted grin, which is better than nothing.

"Hey," I say, trying to make him feel better. "I'm the one who accidentally spanked his monkey to some dude-on-dude action."

"Please explain how you accidentally do something like that and then not tell me about it."

"It was scrambled and the sound was down. In my defense, they totally kind of looked like chicks. Hairy chicks. I thought it was French."

"Wow." Shane pauses for a long time. "I'm really going to miss you, dude."

"Me too." Silence. "So I guess this is what you and Ronnie were arguing about." Shane nods. "Well," I say, "I'm glad you told someone, even if it wasn't me."

"It's not like I didn't want to," says Shane.

"I get it."

"Anyway, she wanted me to tell you. She said you could handle it and she thought you should know before you died."

Shane and I sit in silence again, only now I can hear the ticking of time passing me by, and honestly, it's superannoying.

"Your parents probably expected you a while ago," says Shane. He looks like he might be crying a little, and there's nothing wrong with that.

"Yeah." I know I should go but I don't want to. "Shane . . ."

"I'm sorry I punched you."

"No you're not."

"No," says Shane, "I'm not. I'm still pissed that you're leaving me."

"I know."

Shane stumbles into me and hugs me for real. Not like how guys usually hug each other with pats on the back. "I love you, Ollie. And not in a gay way."

"I love you too, Shane. In any way."

The hug lasts longer than it should but it's cool. Shane could be trying to touch my ass for all I care. He's my best friend and I'll let him go when I'm damn well ready.

Finally I pat Shane's arm to let him go and he yelps. I stumble back a little and he rubs his tattoo.

"Sorry," I say. We both stare at the ground. "So I guess this is good-bye."

Shane pulls off his glasses, wipes his eyes with the back of his arm, and says, "Not so fast, Travers. Just because we got all the mushy feelings out of the way doesn't mean you're done with me."

"What?"

"I'm coming to dinner." He points at his belly and gives me the best grin ever. "This belly still needs food."

I hate to admit it but I feel like I'm emotionally done. Just done. Not done as in I've checked off everything on my list and tied it all up with a neat bow, but done as in I don't know if my heart or soul or whatever you wanna call it can take too much more.

But I'm nowhere near the end. Shane's still tagging along, babbling about what foods he hopes are at dinner, and I've spent like zero time with my parents. And Nana. How can I die without hanging with her?

What I need to do is just suck it up and smile but I feel the same way I did this one Thanksgiving Shane dared me to eat as many pies as I could. I finished a pumpkin and a blueberry. When it came time to do the apple though, no matter how much I wanted to, I felt like I'd explode if I tried.

But it's like GP said, this day isn't all about me. I have to soldier on and let Shane and my family smother me with mushy feelings no matter how much it sucks. So bring it on. And don't forget the pie.

I just hope I can sneak away from my happy family to take care of some "unfinished business" before I die. The way Hurricane left me hanging, I'm like a dangling participle in need of a subject to modify.

Nana hugs me the second I walk in the door. She hugs me so hard I'm not sure she isn't secretly a bodybuilder. "Ollie, how was your day?" she asks, but doesn't give me a chance to answer. "Shane, I should've known." Nana leads Shane and me to the dining room table and sits us down. She's so insistent I'm afraid she'll waterboard me if I don't make with the details, and fast.

"Come on, Oliver, I am not a patient woman. How was your day?"

"It was cool."

"He gets that from you," says Nana accusingly to my mom. "But that's okay, because I know that Shane will tell me everything I want to know. Starting with what happened to Oliver's eye."

If you couldn't already tell, Shane's more than my best friend. He's part of the family whether he likes it or not. I know that after I'm gone, Shane'll still come around to help Nana with the crossword puzzle and fix Mom's computer and steal food. It helps a little to know that with him around, I won't be gone completely.

"It was a minor misunderstanding," says Shane, trying to

dance around the issue. Did I mention that Shane's a terrible dancer?

"Shane popped me in the eye when I showed him my letter," I say.

"Hey! I was upset."

Mom grabs my chin and tilts my face to the side. "I didn't know you had it in you, Shane." I can't tell if Mom's upset that I'll have a black eye for my funeral, or proud of Shane for throwing a solid punch.

"If you think the eye's good," I say with a smile, "wait till you see the tattoos."

Mom and Dad laugh. So do Shane and I, but nervously, because we can't believe they think I'm kidding. Nana, on the other hand, does a good impression of Mom's Look, but she doesn't rat us out.

The whole kitchen is filled with light and love and awesome smells. It's the Disneyland of kitchens.

"What did you guys do today?" I ask. I don't much like being the center of attention where my parents are concerned.

"They went to the courthouse," says Angela. Shane and I both practically jump out of our chairs when the twins sneak up behind us.

"And they got put in jail," says Edith. Then they flash us their evil genius smiles because it's maybe the first time in their short lives that they aren't the ones who got into trouble.

"You did what?"

"It's nothing, dear," says Mom as she dances around my father in the kitchen. It's the first time I've ever seen them cook together. I've seen Mom cook in Dad's kitchen at the restaurant, and I've seen Dad cook in Mom's kitchen, but I've never seen them cook together. It's actually really excellent.

It'd be cooler if I hadn't just seen the look that passed between them that said that whatever happened had something to do with my letter. And that they'd failed. There are always stories about people freaking out and trying to figure out how to reverse a Deathday Letter. No one knows where they come from though and it's ludicrous to try, but I guess they wouldn't be my parents if they hadn't given it a shot.

Dad brings two spoons to the table and hands one each to Shane and me. "Spaghetti sauce à la Travers."

The sauce is delicious. So amazing that I can almost forgive him for this morning's scrambled egg debacle. Spaghetti is my favorite dish my dad makes. I know it's lame. I mean, here's a guy who has cooked for movie stars, and my favorite thing of his is spaghetti. Sometimes you just can't fight who you are.

"Wow, Mr. Travers."

"Best ever," I say, and hand back the spoon. "What else you got in there?"

I make my way into the kitchen. Mom sniffs the air as I get closer, and then sniffs me. "Did you bathe in mint? And vomit? What have you been doing all day?"

Dad puts his arm around my shoulders and guides me out of the kitchen. "We're making all your favorites. Spaghetti, mac and cheese, fried chicken, and not a veggie in sight."

Nana coughs.

"Okay, there are mushrooms in the sauce, but you just said it was my best ever so—"

"It's cool, Dad."

"Right," says Dad. "So why don't you go upstairs and shower. It smells like you've had a busy day."

"And make sure you use a lot of soap," says Nana. "Or bleach."

Mom holds her finger under her nose. "You smell really terrible. Then you can tell us all about your day."

There's that naked feeling again. Mom and Dad and Nana and even Shane are all staring at me, waiting for me to do something, but all I can think is that I'm finally gonna have like twenty minutes of sweet, blessed alone time.

"Shower," I say, pointing upstairs.

"You can use the twins' shower," I say to Shane, and toss him some spare clothes and a towel.

I bound up the stairs and close my door behind me. Alone at last. I'll go back down and spend time with them later, but right now I just want quiet.

My room is exactly as I left it. My comforter is still in a massive heap against the wall and my clothes are all over the floor. It's sad to think that soon my parents will box up all of my junk and give it away. Pieces of Oliver Travers sold on Craigslist.

The face in the mirror isn't even mine anymore. I mean, it's me. Same hair, same eyes, same unfortunate nose, same green hoodie. Maybe a little worse for the wear, especially my eye. But it's still me. Except it's not. It's not me because in order to be someone, you have to grow up and become them, and I'm not grown up yet. I'll never grow up. Never know who I was gonna become.

This reflection is just a ghost. A backward image of someone who's forever frozen as wasted potential.

Robotically, I drag my hoodie over my head and let my shorts fall to the floor, not taking my eyes off the reflection. If I stare long enough, maybe I'll be able to see into the future. Yeah, getting my Deathday Letter gave me the opportunity to do stuff I wouldn't have done otherwise, but that doesn't make it any easier to deal with. In many ways it makes it worse.

Everything that's gone wrong today and the few things that were right swell in my chest and bleed into my fist as suddenly I'm punching the mirror. I'm screaming and putting my fist to the glass and watching it shatter and feeling it cut my knuckles and screaming and screaming and punching.

And I'm on the floor still staring at the not me in the shards of glass. And there's blood everywhere. More blood than glass. But I keep punching 'cause I can't do anything else. I can't put the face in the mirror back together. It's a puzzle now and I don't know what it's supposed to look like, so I just keep hitting.

Until I can't anymore, 'cause Mom's here. Cradling me in her arms like she did when I was a kid and I had a nightmare. I'm not even ashamed 'cause sometimes your mom is the only person in the whole world who can fix a thing, even if it can't be fixed.

"Ollie."

I don't answer. I just sob. Fifteen years old, sitting on my floor not even caring that I'm buck-ass freaking naked, covered in blood and broken glass, crying to my mom.

"I'm sorry I broke the mirror," I say after my sobs turn into great gasping cries and then finally into just embarrassed sniffles.

"I don't care about the mirror," says Mom. "Let me see your hand."

My hand isn't that bad. Little cuts crisscross my knuckles. "It doesn't matter," I say with a laugh. "I doubt this is what kills me."

Mom chokes back a half laugh, half cry of her own. "That's not funny, Oliver."

"It's totally funny."

Mom shakes her head and helps me up. I grab my hoodie to cover myself with. Just 'cause she wiped my butt and changed my diaper and bathed me when I was a baby doesn't mean I want her seeing my bits and pieces now.

I cross my room to the bathroom, expecting Mom to leave, but she tiptoes through the glass and stands in the doorway.

"Your father and I would take your place if we could."

I look into my mom's eyes. They're blue like the eye of a hurricane. I wipe away a tear that's poised on her lash like a high diver. "You really think I'd wanna live without you guys?"

Mom hugs me harder than Nana and Shane combined. "Now you know how we feel."

"But you still have the twins and Nana. And Shane. Sorry, I can't do anything about that one. You're pretty much stuck with him."

"Shane I can handle," says Mom. "But between you and me, when I get my letter, I think those girls are going to be the cause."

I laugh because it's true. "Just wait till they start dating."

"Those little girls dating is the reason I won't let your father own a gun."

My tears are dry and my smell plus my near nakedness is starting to equal major embarrassment.

"Mom?"

"Yes?"

"I should . . ."

"Okay." Mom reluctantly lets me go.

I'm not sure how I'm gonna manage to get away from my parents long enough to die.

"I'll be down in a few."

"Dinner will be ready when you're finished." Mom hesitates in the doorway and smiles. "So long as your father hasn't burned my chicken. I have never met a four-star chef who can't fry chicken."

"Maybe he married you for your awesome chicken-frying skills."

"Maybe," she says. "Or maybe all the other girls just knew better." Mom snickers.

"Thanks, Mom."

Mom chuckles quietly. "So I guess you weren't kidding about the tattoo."

I look down at the inky, bloody bandage hanging off my arm and then back to Mom, trying to look guilty. "Sorry?"

She laughs harder. "We'll let this one slide."

"Not like you can ground me."

"No, I suppose not. But you can at least show me what you got permanently written on your skin."

I pull the bandage off, wincing. "I thought it was appropriate."

"And have you?" asks Mom after scrutinizing it.

"Have I what?"

"Seized your Deathday?"

It takes me a couple seconds to answer but when I do I say, "Not much has gone the way I planned but I'm not sure I would have done anything differently."

Mom stares at my tattoo again and then says, "Well, I'll let you get cleaned up." She turns to leave but as she does I swear I hear her whisper, "I couldn't have asked for a better kid."

Standing in the shower, letting the water run across my face, I feel sorry for Mom. My whole family, really. Including myself. People always talk about how great Deathday Letters are. About how they give people a chance to say good-bye. About how terrible the world would be without them. But I'm not so sure I'm on board with all the warm fuzzies.

Seriously. One day isn't enough time to do anything really meaningful. I wanted to do something so that people would remember me as more than that kid with the funny hair who could stick string up his nose and have it come out his mouth, but what did I really accomplish aside from hurting Ronnie? I stole some clothes and jumped off a bridge and got kicked out of a strip joint without even seeing a real naked girl. Not really the stuff great stories are made of. There should be more. There should be more time. Or less. I shouldn't have wasted the time I had.

And saying good-bye? What a load of shit, man. I think I'd rather have someone tie a hot hook to my intestines and slowly pull 'em out through my navel than spend another second saying good-bye to the people I love. It's torture. I mean, here I am in the shower, and my mom and I just wrung out some sloppy tears and said our see yas, and I have to go downstairs and do it again.

Maybe Deathday Letters should be more of a five-minute warning. Just enough time to say good-bye but not long enough to get too sappy.

The water's cold and I know that I've been in the shower awhile. Everyone's probably downstairs thinking I'm having the longest pull in history, which I'm actually not. I know. Shocker, right? It just doesn't seem as important as it did when I woke up this morning. Or, you know, an hour ago.

It takes me a few minutes to find clean clothes. Normally I'd just throw on whatever's on the floor, but it seems wrong to die in dirty clothes. I mean, what if I die and some hot paramedic's working on me and I have skid marks on my shorts? Not cool.

Shane's already downstairs when I finally join the family. My parents weren't kidding when they said they cooked all my favorites. In fact, I think they cooked every single thing I've ever even hinted that I liked.

"I hope you're hungry," says Nana when she sees me. "I even made pie."

"Lemon meringue?"

Nana looks at me like I'm nuts. "No, pumpkin. Of course lemon meringue. I'm old, not stupid."

"We're hungry," says Angela.

"Can we eat now?" asks Edith.

"I third that," says Shane, rubbing his belly.

"We didn't know when you were coming home," says Dad, "but your mom wouldn't let anyone eat until you did."

"Okay, okay," I say, and take my place at the table. "I feel like I haven't eaten in days."

"Did you not eat today?" asks Mom.

Shane and I look at each other, sharing a grin, and I say, "We ate."

Dad chuckles as he finishes loading up the table with all the plates of food. "I think that whatever they ate managed to find its way back up."

"Girls, listen very closely," I say, and lean toward them. "If anyone ever offers you a soda bottle filled with a little bit of everything from their parents' liquor cabinet, say no."

The twins look at me like I just told them not to shave the cat again, and I get the distinct impression that we've only seen the tip of their evil iceberg. I kind of feel sorry for my parents.

"So, tell me about your day," says Mom.

I look around the table. "I guess it all started when Shane handed me a shovel."

After I finish telling them about the better parts of the day, with a ton of interjections from Shane, Mom tells us how when she was a girl, her family used to have dinner at the table every single night, and that it was her favorite time of the day. We don't get to do that often 'cause Dad's always at the restaurant and the girls are always busy with dance or softball or taking over the world. But I can see what she means, 'cause this may be the best part of my day so far.

Dad tells us stories about when he was in high school. Apparently the twins get their looks from my mom and their fiendish tendencies from my dad. He barely makes it through his story about how he let twenty-nine rats loose in the school numbered one to thirty without laughing. He ended up getting caught on account of he skipped number eleven and that was his number on the football team.

Mom, of course, was a perfect angel in school. Except for the time she set her science class on fire. "Accidentally." Air quotes added by Dad.

Mom and Dad both tell us about their first times drinking. Mom got hammered before her senior prom and fell asleep in her friend's car, missing the whole dance. Dad drank at his house with his buddies and threw up all over Grandpa Lou. Of course he tries to leave out the last part, but Nana clues us all in.

It's the kind of stuff parents don't really tell their kids until they're adults. I tell them pretty much everything I did today, leaving out the stuff about Hurricane and Ronnie, and they're being so cool. Of course, Dad goes into total parent lecture mode when he realizes that we weren't joking about the tattoos. Mom gets him to back off and offers to take me driving in her car, but I decline. I think I've driven enough.

I'm stuffed to my eyeballs. I can tell that everyone's wicked beat as we float to the living room. Mom's head is on Dad's chest, her eyes barely open, the twins are two snoring lumps beside them, and Nana's dozing in the recliner. Even Shane is half asleep. I guess I can't really blame them for taking a little nap.

"I'm glad you had a good day," says Dad.

"Thanks." We sit in silence. "How'd you know?"

"Know what?"

"That I wouldn't go to school today."

Dad laughs and nearly wakes up Mom. "Well, first of all, I know Shane Grimsley." Shane twitches at the sound of his name but a second later he's spooning the couch cushion, drooling up a storm.

"Yeah. He probably would've stuffed me in a sack to get me out of school if he had to."

Dad moves Mom to the other side of the couch and leans her head on the cushion. "And second of all, you're my son. You managed to have more adventures in one day than some people ever do. *Carpe Mortediem* isn't just a tattoo. You lived it."

"But I feel like I didn't really do anything."

"You took chances, Oliver. You took risks. Some people go their whole lives without taking any risks."

My eyes are kind of heavy but there's no way I'm sleeping. "Does that make me a man? I don't feel like a man. I feel scared."

Dad looks like he might cry, which would be bad. I can't handle another tearfest. Luckily, Dad holds it together. He's superglue. "You're more of a man than some men twice your age, Oliver Travers. I can only imagine how you would have turned out, but I know you would've made me proud, because I'm pretty damned proud of you already."

"Thanks?" The whole emotional thing is making me uncomfortable. It's like watching the end of *The Notebook* while reading the end of *To Kill a Mockingbird* while someone punches me in the face. Again.

"I really screwed things up with Ronnie."

"You can fix them." Dad looks at the clock on the cable box. "You have plenty of time."

"I don't know how."

"You'll figure it out."

"I hope so."

Dad smiles at me and messes my 'fro. "Movie?"

I nod. *"Pirates of the Caribbean?"*

"You can never go wrong with Depp."

Dad finds our favorite movie and I find myself thinking more about Ronnie. Or I try to. If there's one thing that can take my mind off of dyin', it's Captain Jack. And, you know, Keira Knightley isn't too tough to look at either. Dad is lights-out before the first fifteen minutes are up.

The thought that this might be the last time I see my family crosses my mind. They're all here, sleeping. Even Shane. And the next time they open their eyes, I might be dead. I don't know how I'm gonna die, but the countdown is in the single digits. It's best to let them sleep.

Anyway, I've done all the good-byes I think I can do and I don't want to do any more. If I have to die, then I want to do it on my terms, surrounded by the people I love. It's been real.

Peace out, yo.

The End

Just kidding. I ain't dead yet and you're stuck with me till I am.

By the way, waiting to die: total yawner. Sorry for having a little fun.

But I sort of mean it. About being done. This whole day has been one big emotional suck. I mean, just look. Here I am, hours from being worm food, and everyone's so drained that they've passed out. Even I'm about crash.

I don't want to sleep though, so the second my eyelids start to get heavy, I check my cell to see if Ronnie's called or texted but she hasn't. Just in case, I go upstairs to the family room and turn on the computer to check my e-mail. I'm not a big Internet guy. Shane's the one who's got a blog and a Web page. Shit, the kid's even got his own YouTube account. There's this really funny one you should check out of him singing "Hot in Herre" with a ukulele. Seriously, just try to imagine a nerdy black dude with thick black glasses, a sense of rhythm that makes me look good, and the voice of a horny dog, rapping with a tiny guitar. Fun-ny. Like watching someone else get hit in the nuts. Or that skateboarding dog.

No mail. That's not entirely true. I do have one e-mail for male enhancement, but since I'm about to be stiffer than a corpse . . . or an actual corpse, I just go ahead and delete it.

All I want is something from Ronnie to let me know that I can still fix things between us. I mean, she knows I'm gonna die, right? Can't she just let it go?

The only thing keeping me from marching over there right now is the likelihood that I'd just make things worse. I mean, how do you tell a girl she gives you more wood than a woodchuck could chuck if a woodchuck could get wood, without sounding like a total tool? I don't know either. I guess if I had the answer, I wouldn't be in this mess.

Shouldn't all the shit I did today have made me wiser? I almost had sex for crying out loud. Doesn't that sort of thing change a man? I still feel like the same dumb kid who woke up this morning and just wanted to polish his scepter. And there are no real answers in my underwear. Except for my name. It's written on the inside of the waistband. Just in case. Dad's a worrier.

I'm so tired my brain begins to wander from making up with Ronnie to making out with Ronnie to how sad she's going to be when I die to how I'm actually going to die. It's not like I have cancer or a tumor or anything, and I don't feel sick. I feel fine. Maybe I'm gonna off myself. Maybe I get so bored that I hang myself. Nah. I can't tie a noose.

Maybe a plane falls through the roof and squishes me. Or maybe the twins finally lose it and take me out. I just hope it's not too painful.

Speaking of the twins, I go back downstairs and gently carry them up to their room, one at a time, and tuck them under their pink comforters. Sleep is the only time they ever look innocent. And even that's a stretch. It's like a matter of degrees, you know? Compared to the Sahara, I'm sure Florida's an absolute icebox. Still, I'm gonna miss them.

"Good-bye, Angela. Good-bye, Edith." I think for a second that they hear me but their eyes stay closed and I just watch them sleep for a while. In their own way, I know my sisters are going to miss me. At least, they'll miss having someone to dress up and put makeup on. Not that I've ever done that. Okay, just the once. Twice. Maybe three times, but that other time *definitely* doesn't count.

"What're you doing?"

I scream like a girl and spin around, slapping Shane as I go. Yes, I slap him. Because I scream like a girl. If you could die from embarrassment, that's what I'd be doing right now.

"Don't sneak up on me like that," I whisper. I look over my shoulder to make sure the twins are still asleep before quietly closing their door.

The second I shut the door, Shane takes his hand away from his mouth and lets the laugh escape.

"Dude, that was the funniest thing I've ever seen in my entire life." He mimes and mocks my scream. "Oh my God, that was funny."

I brush past Shane and head to my room. "It wasn't *that* funny."

"It so was."

"You're a dick."

I stand in my room, not really sure why I'm here. Shane makes himself comfy on my bed, and I don't bother telling him what I was doing there this morning. Payback's a bitch.

"So can I have your comics?" asks Shane after a couple of minutes of watching me stare off into space.

"Already circling my corpse, huh?"

Shane draws circles on my sheets with his finger. "No. I just. You're not going to need them and I thought—"

"I'm kidding, dude. What do you want?"

Shane grins. "Since you asked."

He takes my Xbox games, my comics, some of my T-shirts, and my iPod. I'd assumed I could count on him to take my porn but I guess that's out of the question now. He does, however, promise to get rid of it for me.

I begin making other piles aside from the ginormous one for Shane. There's a stack of stuff Shane's gonna hide from my parents, some things my parents might actually want to keep, like pictures and awards and stuff, a small stack for Ronnie, and even a pile for the twins.

"It just seems like such a shame to get rid of it all." I toss a DVD on the "incinerate immediately" pile. "Bye, ladies, thanks for all the good times."

"You have a problem," says Shane. He grabs the DVD. "*Armagetiton?*"

I shrug. "What? It's the touching story of a giant meteor inhabited by naked alien girls on a collision course with Earth, and the one man with a drill big enough to save them all. Actually, you might like it."

Shane coughs uncomfortably and kicks the pile of Ronnie stuff. It's a pretty small pile. The old yellow *Schoolhouse Rock!* tee she used to wear when she spent the night, a Yeah Yeah Yeah's CD she let me borrow, a Domo stuffed doll, and a book about medieval warfare she gave me for my thirteenth birthday.

"Is this what you're giving Ronnie?"

I nod. "Yeah."

"Kind of lame."

"Yeah." I look at the pile again. "I don't know what else she'd want of mine. Think she'd want the porn?"

"Doubtful."

I grab the medieval book off the pile. "I don't even like knights and shit. Maybe she didn't know me that well at all."

Shane takes the book from me and tosses it back down. "That's not true. You know it's not true."

"But look at this. Music I hate, books I don't like"—I pick up the Domo doll—"and I don't even know what this thing is." I drop it again. "Maybe she was right to break up with me."

Shane sits back on my bed. "You are stupid. I can't say it any plainer. You're a moron."

"Way to kick a dude when he's dead."

"Don't make me slap you." Shane's face goes crazy serious.

"Ronnie doesn't suck at giving gifts, you suck at remembering the things she gave you."

"I don't—"

"For your tenth birthday she took us all go-cart racing. For your twelfth birthday we went to the science museum and she got us the planetarium for a whole hour alone because she knows you love the stars."

I shrug and sit beside Shane. "Okay, so she does know me, then. Maybe I don't know her. I mean, I really screwed up the pudding thing. That should've been gold."

"I told you it was a bad idea."

"I didn't see you coming up with any great plan."

Shane looks at me and sighs. "We've been over this and all this talk of pudding is just making me hungry again."

"Come on, dude, there's got to be something I can do. There's got to be something she wants more than anything else."

Shane's belly rumbles.

"Sorry," says Shane. "But I told you I was hungry."

My brain hurts from thinking and food doesn't sound like a terrible idea. "We've got leftovers to last until 'armagetiton.' Wanna?"

"Get it on? No. Eat food? Absolutely."

We raid the fridge like we didn't just stuff ourselves silly a couple of hours ago. Let me tell you a secret you probably already know: Fried chicken, especially my mom's fried chicken, tastes about a hundred times better as leftovers. I know that a couple hours don't exactly make leftovers, but I won't be around for real leftovers.

I'm standing at the kitchen counter with a chicken leg hanging out of my mouth, and Shane's unceremoniously stuffing his face with an oversize spoon full of mac and cheese when Nana clears her throat.

"Nana," I say. It actually sounds more like "Ehuh," but you get the picture.

"Boys. You didn't think you could eat all the leftovers without inviting me, did you?"

I pull the leg out of my mouth. "Sorry to wake you."

"Just a catnap, Oliver. A stuffed belly will do that to you." Nana looks over her shoulder at the couch. "And I see I'm not the only one." Without missing a beat she takes a hefty slice of lemon meringue pie and sits at the table. "But we're not savages, so get a plate and sit with me."

"Yes, ma'am."

Shane and I fill our plates with more food than we can possibly eat and join Nana.

Nana's pretty old, but I've never seen her look old. Right now, though, she looks like she's got one foot in the grave.

"You look like crap, Nana."

"You have a way with words, kid." Nana takes a bite of her pie. "Let's talk."

"Is this how I die? Are you gonna talk me to death?"

Nana laughs. "You *are* a smartass."

"I'll say," says Shane.

"I'm sorry I'm not going to get to see you grow up, Oliver."

"It's okay, Nana." Here it comes. Cue the violins.

"It's not okay." Nana tries to smile, maybe to reassure me or something, but it's a pathetic excuse for a smile. "I'm petrified of dying, and I've done a lot of living. You shouldn't have to go through this." Nana squeezes my hand. Her skin is like the skin of an apple that's sat on the bottom of the fruit bowl too long. Kind of dry, kind of mushy.

"Nana?"

"Yes?"

"What do you think dying's gonna be like?"

"I don't know, kid. No one does. People who die don't come back."

"Except zombies," says Shane, and then looks surprised, like he didn't mean to say it out loud. I know how he feels.

"Shane Grimsley, can you be serious for one second?" Nana's voice is serious but her face is laughing.

Shane shakes off his expression like it's an Etch-A-Sketch. "How's this?"

"Better," says Nana, rolling her eyes so wildly they go almost all white. Yuck.

"Do you think I'll do all right at it?"

"Dying?" asks Nana. I nod my head. "You're a great kid. The best. And whatever dying is like, I know that you'll do it with honor and dignity, the way you do everything else."

"Except getting tattooed."

I punch Shane in the shoulder and he yelps. "I'm not the one who cried."

"I did not cry."

"Boys," says Nana.

Shane and I both glare at each other. When Nana looks

away, I mouth, *Did so*, but she catches me and corners me with her tired eyes. She has the same eyes as I do, so in a way, it's kind of like seeing what my eyes would have looked like if I hadn't gotten my letter today.

"Not that I don't enjoy Shane Grimsley's company, but shouldn't someone else be here?"

The chicken skin on my plate is suddenly the most interesting thing in the room. "I don't know what you mean."

"You know exactly what I mean, young man."

Oh shit. "Young man" is even worse than Oliver Aaron Travers. I'm pretty sure she's one step away from sticking little pieces of bamboo under my fingernails. Besides, she already knows. It's like she's got ESP: elderly sensory perception.

"Nana, it's nothing."

"Don't 'nothing' me."

"Ronnie was with us and she and Ollie almost kissed because she's still got feelings for him and she feels guilty that he's going to die but then she caught him mostly naked with another girl and he tried to apologize but it wasn't a real apology because it didn't really mean anything and Ollie doesn't get that but he really screwed things up. Sorry, Ollie." The whole thing gushes out of Shane like verbal diarrhea.

I'm flabbergasted. I'd intentionally skipped over that part during the sharing portion of dinner because I didn't want my family to know what a total douche I am. Plus, I don't need my parents or my grandmother thinking about me horizontal. But now Shane's spilled it all out. My secrets are like marbles on the floor and I can't get from one side of the room to the other without tripping over them. So I do the only thing I can think of.

"Yeah, well Shane's gay."

Oops.

The three of us sit around the table staring at one another. I'm pissed at Shane for dumping out my secret and he's not sure what to do now that I've kicked him out of the closet. I'm not even sure what Nana's thinking.

Until she says, "That might have been a shock a few years ago, but we've all known for a while." She pats Shane's hand and smiles.

"You knew?"

"Yes, sweetheart. Even the twins know."

"The twins?"

"I'm afraid so, but we can talk about this later. Right now, we need to talk about how stupid my grandson is." Nana turns the full power of the Deathstare on me. "Tell me everything."

So I do. Leaving no details out. When I finally finish she says, "Oliver, I wish I had more time to teach you about girls, but we'll just have to work with what we have."

"Nana?"

"Do you know why the pudding didn't work?" I shake my head. "Because it wasn't special. If you'd remembered it and thought about it and felt bad about stealing her pudding cups for all these years, then it would have meant something. But you didn't even remember it until today, and only because she told you."

The food in front of me makes me nauseated. "So what do I do?"

"You have to figure that out for yourself."

"It's too late."

Nana smacks me upside the head. "It's not too late until you're dead. You still have a few hours left. Think, Oliver. Don't leave this Ronnie situation unfinished."

"Shane?"

Shane still looks a little peeved that I outed him to Nana, and a little shocked that she and the twins already knew. "I'm with Nana on this one."

"Think, Oliver. Think. You care about Ronnie. What does she want more than anything? What can you do that would say to her that you know her better than anyone else in the entire world? What can you do that would show her how you really feel about her? And think quickly."

It's all down to this, isn't it? I spent most of the day with the girl and I haven't got a clue how to tell her how sorry I am. Not that I almost did another girl, but that I'm dying and leaving her behind. That's what I'm really sorry for, isn't it? If I had the day to do over, I wouldn't not try to get with Hurricane, I wouldn't not dump pudding cups all over her front lawn, I wouldn't not almost kiss her in front of the lighthouse. No, I'm sorry because they're the last moments I spent on this earth with her. I'm sorry because, in spite of how much it hurt her, she tried to help me leave this world a rock star. She tried to help me show the world who OAT really is. And I'm sorry I won't get to do the same for her.

Except maybe I can.

"Get Mom and Dad. We've got some work to do."

Nana smiles and claps her hands. Mom and Dad practically jump off the couch.

"What've you got?" asks Shane.

I run into the kitchen and grab a pen and piece of paper. "Dad," I call. He looks disoriented so I say, "Nana, can you put on some coffee? We've got some planning to do and I need everyone at their best."

Armed with cups of coffee, we gather around the kitchen table like we're planning a war. Everyone's going over the list of stuff I need. I'm not sure how this is all gonna work, but I feel good about it. Like God's up there going, "Sorry I have to kill you, but we can still be friends, right?"

"I don't think this will be impossible, Oliver, but are you sure?"

"Yeah, Dad. You've got to make sure that no matter what, nothing ever happens to it."

"For so long as I live," promises Dad. You know how sometimes people say things like that but they don't really mean them? Like they say to call them anytime but they don't really mean *any*time, 'cause no one wants a call at three in the morning when they're dreaming about naked chicks and guns. Dad means it though. Really means it. I can hear it in his voice. There isn't anything on heaven or earth that he won't do for me.

"Dude, nothing's open this late," says Shane, and turns to my parents. "Did *you* know I'm gay?"

Mom nods. "Your mom and I talked about it—"

"MY MOM KNOWS?" Shane looks like he might puke. "That explains why she keeps trying to take me to see *Rent*."

"Shane!" I snap my fingers in front of his face. "You'll be gay forever, I'll be dead tomorrow, can we focus on what's important?"

Shane nods. "Sorry. It's just . . . my mom . . . Who else knows? The little old man who always checks us out at the grocery store?"

"Yeah, probably," I say. "Back to me."

Once Shane's done having his meltdown, I turn everyone's attention back to the list. "I know it might be tough to get some of this stuff but I absolutely have to have it. It's life-or-death stuff here. Borrow it, steal it, break into the stores if necessary. Then I need you all to set everything up. I know it's a lot to do and you probably won't have much time, but I've got to make things up to Ronnie or die trying."

Mom looks like she's gonna cry and Dad coughs.

"Okay, wrong word. I doubt apologizing to Ronnie gets me killed."

"Unless you do it with pudding again," says Shane. Nana slaps his arm and he cries out. "Damn, Nana."

"We'll take care of it," says Mom. She's practically mainlining coffee and I can hear the jitter in her voice. "I've already called Mrs. Gorey to come over and watch the girls."

"What are you going to do, Oliver?" asks Dad.

"I've got the hardest job of all. I've got to figure out what to wear and then convince Ronnie to come with me."

"Do you think it will work?" asks Nana.

I shrug. "I hope so, 'cause kidnapping her is out of the question. That girl's stronger than she looks."

Silence descends. We all know what we have to do and we all know that if my plan succeeds, I may never see any of them again.

Mom, Dad, and Nana all hug me, and then even Shane gets in on the giant, awkward, painful hug in the middle of my dining room. No one says anything 'cause there's not really anything else to say except, "Hey, guys? Try not to get arrested. Again."

I don't usually worry about what to wear. I'm just not that kind of guy. But just about every single piece of clothing I own is on my bed, and I'm dancing around my room trying to find something to wear and not step on any glass.

Clothes just aren't my thing. I'm the guy who wears socks with sandals. And plaid shorts with a striped shirt. Or brown shoes with a black belt. Why? Because I'd rather be comfortable than stylish.

I could wake up the twins and get them to help me. They have more fashion sense in their ponytails than I have in my whole body. Of course, they'd probably sabotage me. Or I could call Mom. I can just take pictures of what I'm thinking about wearing and she can tell me if I'm color-blind.

But is that how I wanna go out? In an outfit my mom picked for me? I'm fifteen and about to die. I should be able to put together an outfit that says to Ronnie, "Sorry for kickin' the bucket, wanna make out?"

No. That's not what this is about. Sure, I wanna make out with Ronnie. I wanna do a lot more than make out with Ronnie, but right now it's not about making out, it's about making up. About showing her that I'm sorry I'm not gonna be around, that I'm more than just a boy with an eight-cylinder sex drive and hormones that can go from zero to randy in 5.6 seconds.

It's about Ronnie. It's not about me anymore.

Shit. It's been almost an hour. Unless my parents got arrested, they should be setting everything up now. I gotta move.

Jeans. White T. It's the best I'm gonna do. A quick hair check alerts me to the fact that my head looks like an atomic mushroom cloud. It takes me another fifteen minutes to fix it but it's like taming a lion. You can do it, but eventually it's gonna break free and eat your face.

When I'm finally sure that I'm ready, I race out the back door without saying good-bye to the sitter. I feel fired up and just a little scared. But there's hope in the air.

It's only once I'm outside that I realize I haven't got a car. Or any way to get Ronnie. I just assumed I'd have a car. Shane's right—I really am stupid. I can't believe I didn't think about how I was gonna get Ronnie. I seriously doubt she's gonna want to ride on the handlebars of one of my sisters' pink princess bikes.

Shane's house is on the way to Ronnie's and all I can do is pray that he decided not to take his car. Of course, that means waking up his parents to get the spare set of keys, but it's better than spending half the night walking.

As I walk to Shane's house the jitters are eating me alive. No, jitters aren't some strange, tropical bug found in Florida. Those are palmetto bugs. You know. Roaches. That fly.

These jitters are all the doubts grinding around in my belly like broken glass, making me want to hurl. Though I could stand to go the rest of my life without ever puking again. It's just that, what if this doesn't work? What if I show up at Ronnie's house (if I ever get there) and she doesn't want to see me? What if she won't even come to the door? What if I have to explain the whole gory day to her father? Not that Mr. Dittrich is a scary man. I mean, as far as fathers go, Mr. Dittrich is pretty cool.

But she is his daughter. And that's what makes me nervous.

After Ronnie broke up with me, I showed up at her house one night. I'd spent the entire day trying to call her but she refused to answer her phone and I just wanted to talk. After I spent about five minutes yelling up at her window while Shane hid in the bushes, Mr. Dittrich came out and said to me, "I like you, Oliver. You're a nice boy. But if you don't leave Veronica alone, this is going to end badly for you."

It wasn't so much what he said or even the sight of Mr. Dittrich himself that scared the bejesus out of me. Truth is, Mr. Dittrich is pretty goofy-looking with his handlebar mustache and permed hair. He'd have a hard time being scary with a chainsaw and a bloodstained apron. No, it was his lack of smile, the lack of Mr. Dittrich-ness. He was ÜberFather, protector of daughters, and I was the evil menace Ex-boyfriend, potential stealer of virginity.

Hopefully I'll get a little leeway being that I'm freaking dying, but when it comes to daughters, fathers are scarier than the words, "Turn your head and cough."

Thinking about Ronnie and my possible death at the hands of her father, I almost walk right by Shane's house. Miss Piggy is sitting in the driveway right where we left her before we went drinking, and all I can do is mutter, "Thank God," and pray that Shane left the keys in the car.

Shane left me more than just the keys. Taped to the steering wheel is a sheet of paper with a stick-shift diagram and a note that reads: *Thought you might need this. Try not to wreck it.* Best. Friend. Ever. Also a smart-ass.

The door *screeees* and a pudding cup falls out. Damn pudding. I grab it and toss it into the backseat. They're everywhere. The car is a mountain of pudding. What am I supposed to say to a cop if I get pulled over again? I'll be dead in a few hours and I *really* wanted some pudding?

Maybe I should throw it away. I mean, keeping it in the car might remind Ronnie of the shit I said to her or the things she said to me. The stuff about her wishing she hadn't come along and being glad that she'd never see me again. Yeah, those things.

There's no time. Plus, I don't think throwing away the pudding will change anything. It can't change the past and it can't affect the future. It's just pudding.

Miss Piggy snorts to life. Okay, she doesn't really snort, but she sure doesn't roar either. She's like this grumbly bear that chuffs along. Or would if I hadn't just stalled her out trying to reverse out of the driveway.

Mrs. Grimsley peeks out from behind the curtains. She's got a face so sweet it's practically made of cupcakes.

"Please don't come out, please don't come out, please don't come out," I say over and over as I put the car back in neutral and try again. I think I'm sunk when Mr. Grimsley's face appears beside his wife's in the window, but they both just wave at me and disappear. As much as I don't want to deal with them, I know that wave was the last time I'll see them before I die, and that kind of blows.

Luck smiles and I manage to get out of the driveway and down the road without stalling. Seriously, I'm a terrible driver. Maybe I would've gotten better with practice, but I doubt it.

I nearly run through a stop sign before realizing my lights aren't on. But now my windshield wipers are. I wish Shane had left a freaking diagram for this. Oh, God, if a cop sees me now, I'm sure to get arrested.

Nope, now I'm spraying my windshield.

There. Got it. Lights on. Wipers off. Windshield clean . . . er.

I pull up to Ronnie's house and sit in Miss Piggy. I don't know what I'm waiting for. The living room lights are on. Ronnie's lights are on.

My palms are sweaty, I forgot to put on deodorant, and I'm 100 percent certain that this is going to go very badly. She's gonna punch out my other eye. I know it.

I'm not even out of the car before Mr. Dittrich comes out the front door. It's late but he looks like he's been waiting for me.

Mr. Dittrich knocks on the window but I don't roll it down. He's waiting and knocking and saying, "Oliver, roll down the window," but I'm just sitting here, sweating and smelling and praying that the mortician doesn't have to cover up two black eyes.

Screeee!

Mr. Dittrich opens my door and I'm here. I'm now. This is the moment.

"Sir, I just want to see Ronnie. Please don't be mad. I know she doesn't want to see me but I need to see her. There's something I have to show her and stuff I gotta say and I promise that if I've said what I gotta say and she's still mad, then I'll bring her back and die without ever bothering her again, which isn't much of a promise since I'm doomed to die pretty soon but—"

"Oliver. Veronica wants to see you."

That shuts me up.

"She does?" Mr. Dittrich nods. "And you're not out here to stall me while we wait for the police to arrive?"

"No."

"Then why are you out here?"

Mr. Dittrich crouches down so that now he's looking me in the eyes. "To tell you what she won't."

"And what's that?"

"Oliver," says Mr. Dittrich. "I don't want Ronnie to grow accustomed to losing the people she loves."

"She lo—"

"Hush." Mr. Dittrich is quiet for a second. "Deathday Letters are a blessing, Oliver. They give us the opportunity to say things that need saying and do things that need doing. They let us finish some of our unfinished business. But they're cruel, too, because, for people like you and Veronica, they don't give you enough time to finish something that's only just begun. But you try anyway. You try to squeeze all that emotion and all those might've beens into a few hours.

"But you can't. And you'll die trying."

"Sir, I don't get it."

Mr. Dittrich pats my knee. "You'll die soon, Oliver. And if you let her, Veronica will die a little bit with you. You probably can't stop it but I'd appreciate it if you tried."

I'm still not really sure what he's getting at but the seconds are ticking and I don't want to waste any more time, so I just say, "I'll do my best, sir."

Ronnie runs out the door as Mr. Dittrich stands up. She's all bundled up in a ratty old sweatshirt and some jeans.

"You don't have your license, do you, Oliver?"

I shake my head and say, "No, sir, but we're not going too far. And I'll be careful."

"Maybe I should—"

"You're not driving, Dad," says Ronnie as she climbs into the passenger seat. She doesn't even hesitate. It's like she knew I'd come for her.

Mr. Dittrich turns to leave but stops and says, "It's been a pleasure knowing you, Oliver."

I just nod at him. More a shake of my chin. It's not like we ever sat around watching football together, but I guess the fact that I never knocked up his daughter is good enough for him.

I'm actually feeling kind of good. Things didn't go the way I thought they would, but they didn't exactly go south either. Ronnie's beside me, and I still have just enough time to talk to her. Things aren't going too bad at all.

Then Ronnie turns to me and says, "The only reason I'm doing this is because my father said I'd regret it if I didn't, so can we get this over with?" She looks in the back. "I thought we were done with the pudding."

I knew I should have gotten rid of it.

Did you steal Shane's car?"

"Is it considered stealing if he left me the keys and a shifting diagram?"

"No."

"Then no."

We sit at a stoplight in silence. I don't want my plan to implode in the car before I even get a chance to unveil it, so I keep my mouth shut. It's a lot harder to say something stupid if you don't say anything at all.

But it's pretty clear that the silence is making Ronnie uncomfortable. Her hands move from her seat belt to the AC vent, to the hem of her sweatshirt, to her keys, to her phone, and then back to the seat belt.

"Shane taught me to drive after you left."

Ronnie looks up. "Not very well. Light's green."

Ease off the clutch, ease on the gas. No problem. No pressure.

"I got pulled over by a cop."

Not a smile. Not a laugh. Not a twitch. She's just blank. Like the day she broke up with me. Which was chickin' finger day at lunch. I remember 'cause Shane tried to correct the spelling but the lunch dude schooled him. Apparently chickin' is a genetically modified chicken product. Shane and I were discussing all the possible uses for genetically modified chickens, one of which was mounting them with lasers and using them as infantry soldiers, when Ronnie walked up to the table.

We weren't one of those clingy couples that had to sit next to each other at lunch. Even before we dated, sometimes Ronnie sat with us and sometimes she sat with some girls she hung out with in the art room.

I smiled at her and grabbed her hand, but she pulled away. Her cold, blank face clued me in that whatever was wrong was more than her being mad that I'd been playing Halo with Shane while I was on the phone with her two nights ago. It was like she'd taken an eraser and scrubbed her face clean of all her emotions.

She told me it wasn't gonna work out. Just like that. I don't think I said another word for the rest of lunch. I don't even remember my classes after that.

And that's how she looks right now. I can't tell whether she just doesn't care that I'm dying or whether it's so much that she's just blown a fuse.

214

I keep driving. It's all I can do.

It's only a few minutes, but it feels like hours. It's funny because I have a feeling my last few hours will feel like minutes.

"Are we going to your dad's restaurant? Some stupid candle-lit midnight snack isn't going to fix this, Ollie."

Not talking. Not me. Nope. Not gonna say a word. I look at her quickly and whisper a prayer that she doesn't decide to jump out the window.

"Predictable," says Ronnie as we pull into the lot of Caroline's. Dad named it after Mom. She hates it and has spent a considerable amount of effort trying to get him to change it. "It's always about food or sex with you, isn't it?"

I resist explaining to her for the millionth time that it really is always about food or sex, but it's not our fault. I'm passing that torch to Shane. It's a battle he'll never win but it's a war we have to keep fighting.

The lights inside are on. Dad must be doing what I asked.

Miss Piggy idles. She's grumpy, I think. She chugs and shudders, chugs and shudders. I don't think she's used to so much driving in one day.

"Let's do whatever lame-ass thing you have planned, Oliver. Some of us have school tomorrow."

"Ouch."

I catch a glimpse of a crack in that blank face of hers. Ronnie's in there somewhere. I just have to dig her out. Good thing I have that shovel Shane gave me.

Ronnie pushes open her door and walks around to the front while I turn off the engine. All my insecurities crush me like one of those wicked machines they have at the junkyard that turns perfectly good cars into cubes. That's me. A twisted metal cube of wuss. But it's not really being wussy if my fears are founded, right? I mean, this could tank the same way Plan Pudding did. I could say the wrong thing again and screw it up.

Get your head in the game, Travers. There are a thousand ways to screw this up, and if I don't concentrate, I'll lose Ronnie forever.

"I haven't got all night," says Ronnie from the hood of the car where she's waiting.

The night is actually about all I have.

I get out of the car and say to Ronnie, "You ready?"

Ronnie sighs. "Ready to be underwhelmed? Ready to be annoyed? Ready to leave? Yes. All of the above."

I hold out my hand for Ronnie to take, but she shakes her head, stands up straight, and heads for the door. I let her get all the way there before I say, "We're not going inside."

Then I start walking. I don't look back to see if she's following because I know she is. She'll probably stand at the door for half a second because, even though she said she wasn't, she was kind of hoping for a romantic meal with two plates of beautiful food and some nonthreatening alternative ballads with candlelight and flowers and nice tablecloths. None of which I have. Then her curiosity will get the best of her and she'll follow. She'll follow because she needs to know what plan I've managed to brew in my soupy brain that she didn't anticipate. That's who Ronnie is. She thinks she knows what's gonna happen, and she preemptively insulates herself from the imagined fallout.

But that's not gonna happen here. I won't let it.

I shove past the bushes and around the side of the building where the Dumpsters and grease traps are. The smell is warm and familiar. And gross. I keep going past the Dumpsters though, until I'm at the back of the building. The back of the building faces the road that leads to the MFEI Bridge. Our bridge.

And I wait.

"Ollie?"

Ronnie lets me take her hand this time. Probably 'cause of the dark. The reason doesn't matter.

The stars are pretty awesome though. Come on, I gotta be a little grateful that I'm not dying on a day where the forecast calls for thunderstorms. I mean, if you've gotta die, and I'm not saying I recommend it or anything, doing it on a day as beautiful as today is pretty sweet.

We're not here for the stars, though.

"Ronnie."

"Ollie?"

"I know you kind of hate me right now."

"I don't h—"

I turn to Ronnie and put my finger to her lips. "Yeah. You do. Maybe not for the reasons you think you do, but you do."

Ronnie drops my hand and shoves me away. "I'm mad at you because you're a jerk."

"Okay. True. I'm a jerk. But you're not mad at me for that."

"No?"

"No." I take both of Ronnie's hands this time. "You've always known that I'm kind of a jerk. In the same way that *all* dudes are jerks." She wants to pull her hands away but I don't let her. "You're mad at me 'cause I'm dying."

"That's ridiculous."

"And because you dropped everything to try to help me leave my mark on the world."

"Ollie, don't."

"And that didn't include leaving my mark on some random girl we met at a drug dealer's house. You wanted me to leave my mark on you."

"I most certainly did not—"

"That came out wrong."

"I'll say."

My stomach starts to sour. I'm screwing this up. "I fucked up, Ronnie. Not for hooking up with Hurricane but for not seeing what you were trying to do. And the only way I know how to apologize is to help you the way you tried to help me."

Ronnie's mouth opens but before a single word gets out, floodlights barge into the night and light up the place. Ronnie covers her eyes with her hands and slowly takes them away, blinking in the almost bright enough to be midday light.

"What is this?"

I shift Ronnie so that she's staring at the freshly cleaned brick wall. "There's no tablecloth, no food, no silverware, no candlelight. What I've got is a blank wall, a drop cloth, paint, paintbrushes, and you. Oh, and music." I snap my fingers and a song comes on that I know Ronnie will instantly recognize.

"Is this what I think it is?"

"The mix you made for Shane and me when we both had our tonsils out."

Ronnie smiles. Briefly. So briefly you'd need a superspecial camera to capture it, it's that fast. But it's another crack, so I'll take it. Then she says, "I don't get this, though. Ollie?"

I let go of one of Ronnie's hands. The paints are stacked to the side, along with brushes and ladders and things I'm pretty sure weren't even on the list. Seriously, my family is full of rock stars.

"It's a wall."

"I get that, I'm not stupid. It's a wall. But what are we doing here?"

"You sacrificed your feelings today to help me cross shit off my list. Well, mostly off Shane's list, but you get the point. So before I die, I want to help you cross something off your list. I wanna help you make *your* mark on the world."

I let go of Ronnie's hand, walk over to the pile of supplies, and get her a paintbrush. "Go on, Ronnie. Make your mark on the world."

Ronnie looks at me and then to the bridge behind us in the distance. The same bridge we jumped from. "But, Ollie," she says. "It's just a wall."

"It's a place to start."

Ronnie holds the paintbrush. It shakes in her hand. "I can't do it alone."

"Yeah you can."

"I don't want to do it alone."

"I won't leave until I have to."

Ronnie runs her fingertips over the brush and closes her eyes. I don't know what she's doing—remembering something, maybe? All I know is that she's more peaceful than I've ever seen her. It's like she's doing something she was always meant to do. I almost feel like an intruder, like I shouldn't be here, but I'm glad I am.

We're beyond words right now. Ronnie's so small, I just want to collect her in my arms and kiss the sadness away. But this isn't my moment; it's Ronnie's.

Plus, my parents and Nana are staring at us from around the corner, giving me a big thumbs-up, and Shane's right behind them with his freak show–crazy grin.

I smile and wave them away. Wave them good-bye.

"So, what do you want to paint?"

Ronnie straightens. She's not small anymore. She doesn't need my help. Even if she says she does. "Ollie, I don't—" Ronnie turns around, looking into the night.

Then she begins and I just follow her lead. It's a bit like dancing that way, but not the awkward, lock-kneed kind we did in eighth grade. This is like a waltz.

My parents are gone. Shane's gone. It's just me and Ronnie and the wall.

You're really terrible at this," says Ronnie as she watches me at the top of the ladder. "You're holding the brush like it's going to bite you."

I look behind me and hold the paintbrush over Ronnie's head. She stares up at the drop of yellow paint just daring it to drip. Of course, I pull back before it does. Because I'm not stupid.

"Maybe I wouldn't suck so hard if you'd tell me what I'm painting."

Ronnie steps back and looks at the wall, then at me, and then back at the wall. "Just get back to work, Travers."

The truth is that even knowing what Ronnie's inspiration is, I'm not sure how the swath of blue under a gray arch trailing a yellow blob is ever going to look like anything. Right now, to me, it's just a mess of paint. I guess that's why Ronnie's the artist and not me. Besides, watching Ronnie move across the wall is like watching a ballet. Yes, I've actually seen a ballet. It was pretty amazing once I got over the nausea-inducing softball-size bulges in the dude dancers' tights. One graceful move led to another and another and a lift and a twirl and that move where they stand on the tips of their toes. Each part of the dance, if taken separately, was beautiful but incomplete.

That's how Ronnie's wall is. I don't know how it's all going to add up, but I know that it will. And it's going to be way cool.

"How did you know I could paint?" asks Ronnie. "I never told you guys." We've switched places and now she's on top of the ladder and I'm standing at the bottom, staring up.

"I've seen some of your stuff in the art room." I laugh. "I never really thought of you as a real artist. Well, not until now. Honestly, I just thought the idea of it would be cool. You know, make your mark on the world and all."

Ronnie's body shakes with a laugh. "So it was just another stab in the dark?"

"No," I say. "It wouldn't have mattered if you'd come out here with me and painted stick figures on this wall."

"It would have mattered to me."

"Why?"

"Because I want this to be perfect."

I take the paintbrush from Ronnie and hand her a smaller one. "Well, that's just silly."

"It's not silly."

"It's definitely silly," I say. Ronnie stops painting and looks down at me. "This doesn't have to be perfect. No one's perfect. Look at me. If today was my wall then I pissed all over it."

"Today wasn't so bad, Ollie."

I cock my head to the side and say, "Today was a wreck."

"Not all of it."

"Okay. Not all of it." I breathe deeply and get Ronnie some more paint. "The point is that today wasn't perfect. Today was a wall full of pornographic stick figures." Ronnie starts to argue with me again but I don't give her the chance. "But they're *my* pornographic stick figures, and I'm damn proud of them."

We fall silent and into our work again.

A few minutes later Ronnie says, "Maybe your wall was marked up with porno stick figures today, but tonight it's the Sistine ceiling. And that makes it perfect to me."

I lean my head against Ronnie's leg. "So I guess I'm not so terrible at this after all?"

Ronnie points to the wall with her brush. "At this? No, you're a wreck. But for the rest I'd say that you're definitely getting better." Ronnie blushes under the bright lights, and as if to cover her embarrassment, she takes the paintbrush and slaps me on the cheek with it, leaving a patch of green in my peripheral vision.

"Oh, it's on!" I sprint to the paint cans, get a brush dipped in blue, and fling it at Ronnie as she leaps off the ladder and runs.

"Watch the wall," she yells, though she's mostly giggling.

I whip a wide arc of paint in her direction and watch it splatter across her torso.

Ronnie clutches her chest and falls to her knees. "I'm hit. Ollie, I'm hit." She holds out her hands and they're covered in blue.

"Score!" I go to Ronnie to help her up and she ambushes me with her brush, smearing paint right up my neck and under my chin.

"Even?"

"Barely." I drop the brush and go in for the tickle. Ronnie's deceptively strong and she wriggles around so that, before I know it, she's on top of me with her fingers in my armpits and under my knees and against my ribs. I squirm and laugh and scream for mercy but she's relentless. I attempt a counterattack but Ronnie's defenses are impenetrable.

"Mercy! MERCY!"

Ronnie drops on top of me and she's breathing so hard she can barely speak. "That was fun."

"For you."

"You liked it," says Ronnie, and winks at me.

"Maybe a little."

We lie on the ground and stare up at the sky. The floodlights make it difficult to see the stars, but neither of us moves.

"Hey, Ollie?"

"Yeah?"

"If you hadn't gotten your letter, what do you think you would have grown up to be?"

Silence follows because I don't know what to say. Ronnie takes that to mean something else and immediately apologizes. "Sorry, Ollie, I just . . . I didn't mean to make you think about . . . I just . . ."

After a few moments I say, "No, that's okay. I thought about it."

"And?"

"I wanted to be a lot of things. A chef like Dad, an astronaut, a fireman, a professional video gamer."

"What about everything else?"

"Like, did I think about going to college and getting married and having a litter of kids and a mortgage and going bald and getting fat?"

"Something like that." Ronnie's voice is soft.

"Not seriously. And not 'cause I'm the kind of guy who lives each moment like it's his last, but because I was always afraid of the future. The future was something that would happen later. Mostly I just wanted to get through the day without drooling on myself."

"I didn't mean to bring it up."

I smile at Ronnie. "Nah, it's cool. But now I'm glad I didn't waste a butt load of time thinking about the future."

"Doesn't that make you angry though? That your future's being taken away from you?"

"Maybe. But I think that if I'd had a future, I probably would have found a way to botch it. Besides, getting my letter brought you back into my life. So, that's a plus."

Ronnie sits up and says, "Do you remember that game we used to play in middle school?"

"Dodgeball?"

Ronnie shakes her head.

"Name That Hooker?"

Ronnie laughs silently. "Definitely no."

"Then I don't remember."

"Come on. The Vagina Game? Where you fill in movie titles with the *V* word?"

I sit up beside Ronnie. "You always hated that game. Said it was demeaning."

Ronnie motions for me to come closer. "Can I tell you a secret?"

"Who am I gonna tell?"

"Good point." Ronnie looks around like she's making sure we're alone. "I only pretended to hate that game. When you guys played it, I'd yell at you, but secretly I'd write my favorites in a spiral notebook when I got home."

"You big fibber." My grin busts out. "I can't believe you never told me. So what have you got?"

"Now?"

"No, tomorrow. Of course now."

Ronnie screws up her face in concentration. "No Country for Old Vaginas."

"Not bad," I say with a chuckle. "How about The Time Traveler's Vagina."

Now we're both laughing. "Hellboy II: The Golden Vagina," tosses out Ronnie.

"Indiana Jones and the Kingdom of the Crystal Vagina."

Ronnie's practically howling and she can barely speak. "Charlie and the Chocolate Vagina." She throws her arms around my neck and her laughter begins to sound like crying.

"Ronnie?"

"Nothing. No. I'm fine."

I put my arms around her and let her laugh even though I really do think she's crying.

When Ronnie finishes, she pushes me away and stands up. "We should finish the wall." She smoothes her shirt and gets her brush.

"Yeah." I follow her back and look up at the wall again.

Ronnie climbs the ladder and begins to paint again. I grab a rag and try to wipe my cheek and neck clean. When I finish, Ronnie's staring at me from her perch.

"Pirates of the Caribbean," she says, "Dead Man's Vagina."

0:17

The air is thick and wet. The cars drive by, their head-lights blinking like their drivers, who are awake on this early morning, trying to clear the crumblies from their eyes. The world is a wonder, a sleeping dog trying to breathe its first breath of the morning.

But Ronnie and I aren't in that world. We're in a world of intoxicating paint smells, of brushes that *shuuuu-shuuuu-shuuuu* as Ronnie drags them across the brick wall, of freakishly bright floodlights.

I feel like I could live forever at this wall, in this second, with Ronnie and the paints. This second is better than sex. I don't really have any frame of reference, but that doesn't matter. I just know. I know it in the same way I know that

Ronnie's gonna need a new, smaller brush with the blue paint.

But the next second I'll hear the rustling of the leaves as the wind from the ocean blows the day in. The day that will take me away from this second and Ronnie and our world made of brick and paint and halogen light.

The outside world filled with wonder and beginnings, and my world of death and endings, are about to collide. But for one more minute I stare at Ronnie, sitting at the top of the ladder, one brush in her mouth, one in her hand. Her sweatshirt is a patchwork of paint stains and strands of paint-flecked hair are tucked behind her ear.

I could die right now. This is one of those perfect moments in life. Like family dinner, or drinking with Shane. A moment where life and death and pudding and girls named Hurricane don't matter even a little. It's one of those perfect moments where only the people in it matter, and that's Ronnie and me.

Except I can't die here. This is Ronnie's moment. I get what Ronnie's father was trying to tell me. She *would* die with me a little if I let her. Because that's what memory is. If I died now, every time she came to this wall, she'd die too. So this moment has to belong to her. She can't die for me. I have to live for her. Not really live, that's not gonna happen. I have to be alive in this moment for her, so that every time she comes here, to her wall, I'll be here with her. Alive.

Which is why we have to go.

The sun's not up yet. I don't know what time it is, but I know that my time's about up.

I can't hide anymore and I know it. It's like the time I got a

D in Geometry, which wasn't my fault. There should be a rule that all high school teachers should be older than sixty and not have an awesome rack. Anyway, I hid that report card as long as I could, enjoying my freedom in that space where my parents didn't know. I was aware that eventually I'd have to face the consequences, and as that time drew near, time became this tangible thing, a noose pulling tighter.

The funny thing is that the closer my death gets, the calmer I feel. Not at all like Geometry. Oh, I'm still afraid. Afraid of dying badly, afraid of all the things I won't get to finish, afraid of what is or isn't waiting for me after death. But I just know that I can't run any farther. There are no more bridges to jump off, no more lighthouses to hide in, no more girls who aren't Ronnie to almost have sloppy sex with. It's just me and the end of my life.

And Ronnie. Always Ronnie.

"Ronnie?"

She looks down from what she's doing. There's a smile on her lips that hasn't left in hours.

"Huh?"

"Can you come down here?"

Ronnie looks at me and then the wall, and sighs. "You need to go home." It's not a question. Maybe she can feel time as acutely as I can.

But I shake my head. "No. There's one last thing I wanna do and it's not on anyone's list."

"What is it?"

"I've never seen the sunrise from the beach."

Ronnie cocks her head to the side like the idea of me wanting to see the sunrise is as strange as a roast beef sub without any mayo. But a guy can appreciate a little nature on the last day of his life, can't he? I'm just sayin'.

Plus, there's still so much I need to say to Ronnie, things she may not want to hear, and the beach, the sunrise, feels like the right place for that.

"Whatever you want, Ollie." She starts packing up her brushes, but I take her hand. "I'm not sure we have time for that."

She checks her phone. "Right. Sun rises soon." But I wasn't talking about that. "Do you think we can make it in time?"

"I hope so."

"Then we should hurry." There's a tear balanced on her eyelid. But this isn't the place for tears. Not those tears. This is a happy place. Ronnie's place. And I'll always be here waiting for her.

We both face the wall and all the pieces have come together. It's Ronnie and Shane and me, frozen in time as we jump from the bridge. It looks like we could leap right out of the wall. Even though Shane's face is frozen in that epic scream of his, we're all smiling. And *Carpe Mortediem!* is written down my arm, even though I wasn't inked when we jumped. It's all there. The water and the bridge and Officer Tubby. There's even a small ship in the water that somehow kind of looks like a certain part of the female anatomy. It's still unfinished but I can see it. I know how it ends.

"It's beautiful, Ronnie."

"I didn't get to finish."

"Most people never do. But you will. I know it."

* * *

We drive to the beach in silence, which is okay with me. I've managed not to screw things up thus far, and if you don't mind, I'd like to keep it that way.

I'm not much of a morning person. Usually if I'm up before dawn it's to take a leak and then crawl back into bed. But I've seen my share of mornings. Enough to know that they're usually bright and loud and damp.

I'll admit though, and maybe it's just 'cause I know I'm never gonna see another morning as long as I live, I'm totally in love with this morning.

It could have something to do with the fact that Ronnie's here with me. Maybe. Just a little.

And I know she's feeling it too.

Miss Piggy's windows are down and I can hear the birds doing their whole "Look at my feathers" song and dance. At least I guess that's what they're singing about. What else do birds have to sing about except for their feathers or eggs or nummy, nummy worms?

It almost makes me wish I'd taken the time to see more dawns instead of playing Whac-A-Mole under my covers. Almost. Still, I have *this* time left and I'm not gonna squander it. I breathe it all in.

Ronnie smiles at me as I park on the side of the road. She's a mess. Wow. I seriously think there might be more paint on her than on the wall.

"Why are you laughing?" she asks.

I lick my thumb and try to wipe some of the paint off of her cheek but it's not coming off. "No reason." But I can't help laughing.

"I think we missed the sunrise."

My laugh falls silent. Maybe I missed my moment.

"Maybe there's still some left." Ronnie practically jumps out of the car. "Come on!"

I open my door and freak as a car with its horn blaring passes, swerving into the other lane to avoid my door. Which is sticking out into the road. Because I'm an idiot.

"Nice one, Ollie," says Ronnie, and she takes off toward the water.

I check to make sure there are no more cars, and get out. Caught up in Ronnie's smile and laugh, I chase her down the sand. One of my shoes flies off but I don't even care. It's just a shoe.

I'm sweaty and out of breath by the time we reach the edge of the water, which doesn't say too much for my general state of fitness. It's like a twenty-second sprint. But the water tickles my toes and I'm reborn.

The sun is half up. I can't believe I've never seen this before. You know how the Greeks thought that some blond dude in a chariot was the one who made the sun rise? Yeah, well that's bullshit. It's Ronnie. She's the one who makes the sun rise with her smile and her laugh. They pull the sun through the sky the same way they pulled me out of Shane's car and down the beach.

We watch the sun until it's all the way up and we're just two people being bathed in its light.

"You know I'm sorry, right?"

"It's not your fault," says Ronnie.

"Really?"

"You didn't send yourself a Deathday Letter."

"Oh. Right. I actually meant about Hurricane, but if we're not talking about that, then I'm totally good."

Ronnie turns to me. "I can't be mad at you for that. I am, don't get me wrong, but you are who you are."

"But that's *not* who I am, Ronnie. I would have waited for you forever. I just thought you didn't want me anymore." I can feel the tear in the corner of my eye and I don't care. Maybe that makes me a wuss, but at some point every guy's gotta man up and admit he's got a soft spot.

"I always wanted you, Oliver. But you turned into this other person when we dated. You never wanted to talk anymore. All you wanted to do was make out. And you talked about sex all the time. There was all this pressure."

I kick at the sand with my one socked foot. "Trying to get laid is like a biological imperative. I can't help it. Shane can explain it better. But it doesn't mean I don't love you."

"Do you even know what that means, Ollie? Because I'm not sure I do."

I hook my thumbs in my pockets and feel the corner of my letter poking out. "I think I do. It's confusing. There are two of you."

"Are you still high?"

"It's not like that. One day you stopped being Ronnie and you started being Veronica. Veronica's this beautiful, awesome, amazing, untouchable girl. But Ronnie's my best friend. I just didn't know how to reconcile the two. I love Ronnie the way I love Shane but I love Veronica in a way that makes me feel like I'm being turned inside out."

"But I'm the same person," she says. "It's all me."

"Damn it, Veronica, you know I'm not good with this kind of stuff. You're my best friend, you always will be, but you're also the girl I'm head over heels, jump off a bridge for, madly in love with. And when you broke up with me, it tore me apart."

Ronnie looks like she wants to take my hand but she doesn't. "I'm not ready for this now, I wasn't ready for it then. Ollie, that's why I broke up with you. This, us, it's all too confusing. I hoped that one day we'd get to try again. This is so unfair." Ronnie's about to lose it.

"Veronica." I take her chin in my hand. "I. Love. You. Maybe I don't know what that means, and maybe you don't either, but I know how it feels. It feels like I'm tied in knots and I'm on fire and that I have so many feelings that I just can't contain myself."

I pull Ronnie to me. Without fear or hesitation. "I know you feel it too. I saw it in your eyes on the bridge."

Her body is warm against mine and she's staring right at me with her green eyes. They're like bloodstones, rusty and green.

"Tell me what it was like," Ronnie says.

"Driving? Getting tattooed?"

"No."

"What?"

"Kissing Hurricane."

I thought we weren't talking about Hurricane but my thoughts drift back to that kiss.

"It was kind of wet. Really wet. And toothy."

"Did you like it?"

"Eh. It was okay."

Veronica giggles. "That doesn't sound good."

"Well, she kind of attacked me. It's not really an experience I'd care to repeat."

Veronica's head droops and she kicks at the sand. "So she wasn't better than me?"

"Definitely not. You're like in the major leagues of kissing and she's one step above the Special Olympics."

"Don't be mean," says Ronnie, and she slaps my shoulder for good measure.

"Ow!"

"You deserved that." Ronnie smiles and gets even closer. "How about we see if I can erase the terrible memory of Hurricane."

"Yes, please."

"And I promise not to attack you."

I stutter and shake. "That'd be awesome."

Ronnie closes her eyes and I close my eyes and our faces inch together. I can feel her breathing and I can almost taste her lips. Then I miss and kiss her nose.

"Sorry," I say, and try to keep from laughing.

Veronica doesn't even try. She's laughing harder than I've seen her laugh all day.

"So, you do know it's mean to laugh at a dude with a Death-day Letter 'cause he's a crappy kisser?"

Ronnie winks at me. "You're not a crappy kisser. You're just out of practice. Let's fix that."

Veronica grabs my hand and pulls me to her and kisses me. And it is *nothing* like kissing Hurricane.

Time stops. Not literally, but close enough. We're unstuck in time with our lips pressing against each other's. I've kissed Ronnie loads of times but this is different. Her lips are warm and soft and she wraps her arms around my waist and I pull her as close to me as I can, like I'm trying to absorb her body into mine.

This is how kissing should be. I could be wrong and I'll never get the chance to know, but maybe kissing's only good when it's with someone you really love.

I never want to stop kissing Veronica Dittrich. I want to kiss her until the world ends and then just a few seconds longer.

And then it ends. Not the world. The kiss. But it could be the world for all I care.

She brushes my face with her hand. "I don't want you to die."

The sun is in the sky. The day is born. It's tomorrow.

"Veronica. This moment, this second, this is us. You and me."

"You're not making any sense."

"I love you, Veronica Dittrich. I need you to know that."

There's so much to say, too much to say. I want to tell her that she's the most important thing that ever happened to me. I want to tell her that every night before I went to sleep, it was her that I thought about, and that every time I walked the halls and she wasn't with me, I looked for her. And that what she did for me today made it okay for me to die.

I want to tell her there's nothing else I need before I die. Sure, there's loads of stuff I could do, loads of stuff I'd like to do, but I'm happy. Right now, I'm as happy as I've ever been, and I can't imagine living a thousand lifetimes and ever being happier than I am right this second.

I need to tell her that this is our perfect moment. So that she'll remember me and remember that she loved me, but know that I couldn't have died happier.

But I'm not that guy. I'm not articulate like Shane. I'm the guy who sticks his foot in his mouth. Who dumps pudding on a girl's front lawn because he thinks that's an apology. I'm not the guy who tells the girl he loves that he's perfect and she's perfect and this is a perfect moment.

I'm the guy who just says, "Thank you," and kisses Veronica again. Only it's not a soft kiss. It's a hard kiss. It's my lips mashed to hers and her tears and my spit and the sounds of two people who want to carve out a hole in the moment and live there forever.

And Ronnie. Ronnie's the girl who knows. She's the girl who says, "I love you, Oliver," and grabs my ass.

I say "I love you" back and let my vision blur into my tears, trying not to drip snot onto her sweatshirt. And, "Please don't let my parents show naked baby pictures of me at the funeral."

Then we just exist. I'm still alive. She's gonna be alive for a long time. But this time we're alive together. I don't know for how much longer but I'm okay not knowing.

"Ollie?" says Ronnie.

"Yeah."

"Don't you want to know why?"

"Why?"

"Why you? Why now?" Ronnie's voice is barely above a whisper.

I look around at the sun and sand and sky and the blue, blue ocean. "Nah. I'm good."

Which makes Ronnie chuckle.

I squeeze Ronnie's hand. It's dry. She's not afraid anymore, and neither am I. "We should get—"

"I know."

But we don't. Not right away. We soak it up for another few minutes until I know that a few minutes are all I have left.

I lead Ronnie back to the car.

Miss Piggy gleams majestically in the sun.

"I can't believe you got a tattoo."

I stop as I'm about to open Ronnie's door. "Of all the things we did today, that's the one thing that shocks you?"

Ronnie shrugs. I open her door. A stray pudding cup falls out and rolls into the street. Ronnie laughs.

"Stupid pudding," I say, and kick it under the car and into the road. "When the world ends it's just gonna be Twinkies, roaches, and those damn pudding cups."

"I can't believe you really thought that would make me not mad at you."

"I was high."

"I'll say. How many of those things did you buy, anyway?"

"I lost count."

"Well, we can't leave it." Ronnie moves to get it but I stop her. "Let me," I say. "You don't even like pudding, remember?"

I take Ronnie's hand and kiss it.

I walk around the front of the car and stop at the line.

Ronnie says, "My hero."

I turn my back to the road and bow.

I spin into the road to get the pudding.

Horns.

Squeals.

Tires.

Screams.

Sirens.

But the last things I hear are the words "I love you, Oliver Aaron Travers" from Ronnie's lips, and that's pretty freakin' cool.

ACKNOWLEDGMENTS

The Deathday Letter exists thanks to the legion of monkeys on typewriters I keep chained in my basement. They're currently hard at work on my next book: AKJDFJKLDSNEN!

Seriously.

The following people were also responsible for bringing my book to print. And by responsible, I mean you should blame them if you hate it.

My awesome agent, Chris Richman, deserves a world of thanks for believing in my ability to build an entire book around death and penis jokes. Without him I'd still be sitting in front of my computer stalking agents on Twitter.

Huge thanks go out to Anica Mrose Rissi who helped me strip away the fat and find the real heart of this book. Even if she doesn't like *Glee*.

Thanks to Emilia Rhodes for being my patient guide through the editing process and for helping me smooth out the many rough edges, but not for taunting me with banana pudding that never materialized.

To Sammy Yuen Jr. for putting together a cover that my fourteen-year-old self would totally not be embarrassed to read.

To my amazing copyeditor, Jenica Nasworthy, for keeping my subjects and verbs in agreement, and for trying to put my dinosaurs where they belong.

To the entire staff at Simon Pulse who busted their butts to help make this the best book possible. I haven't met most of you yet, but when I do there'll be pudding for everyone!

To Rachel Melcher for being my first and best reader all the way back to the days when I sent her pages via fax, and for being the Shane to my Ollie.

To Ryan Hutchinson for filling my childhood with all the horrific experiences that I now get to spin into stories. It's cheaper than therapy.

To my family for being so weird.

To Angela Englata for her unconditional support and boundless excitement, and for always being there when I come out of my hole.

Thanks to The Tenners who kept me from freaking out during revisions.

To all my awesome friends who have stood with me and endured my constant rambling about this and other books, and who put up with me disappearing or not answering my phone for weeks at a time.

And finally, a special thanks to the annoying, yappy dogs in the apartment across from mine for teaching me that I really can write through anything.

ABOUT THE AUTHOR

Shaun David Hutchinson was born and raised in an uptight beach town in South Florida where he wasted his days sleeping in class, reading anything except what he was assigned, and toy shopping with his best friend.

Living once again in the aforementioned uppity beach town with his dog, who is both blind and totally insane, Shaun hopes to accomplish a long list of goals—like visiting every country on the planet and running through Tokyo in a Godzilla costume—before he receives his own Deathday Letter.

NEED
A DISTRACTION?
READ ON THE EDGE WITH SIMON PULSE.

DAN ELCONIN

TOM LOMBARDI

TODD STRASSER

LYAH B. LeFLORE

HANNAH MOSKOWITZ

ALBERT BORRIS

PETER LERANGIS

THOMAS FAHY

Published by Simon & Schuster

YOU HAVE BEEN CHOSEN.
YOUR INITIATION STARTS NOW.

THE RECRUIT

AND LOOK FOR YOUR NEXT MISSION:

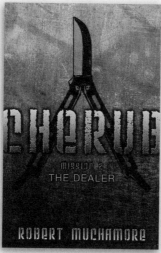

THE DEALER

FROM SIMON PULSE | PUBLISHED BY SIMON & SCHUSTER

The road less traveled might just be the ride of your life!

TAKE ME THERE
Carolee Dean

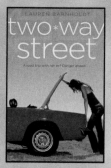

TWO-WAY STREET
Lauren Barnholdt

CRASH INTO ME
Albert Borris

DRIVE ME CRAZY
Erin Downing

THE MISSION
Jason Myers

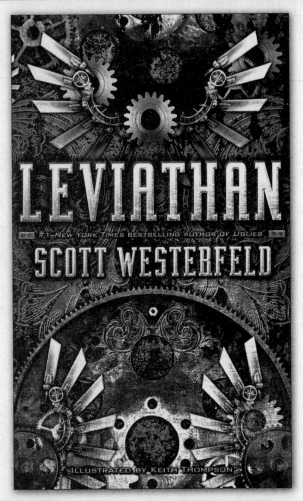